Welcome to Suite 4B!

Gone to the stables

Jina

Shh!! Studying—
please do not disturb!

Mary Beth

<u>GO AWAY!!!</u>

Andie

Hey, guys!
Meet me downstairs in the
common room. Bring popcor

Join Andie, Jina, Mary Beth, and Lauren for more fun at the Riding Academy!

And coming soon:

After dinner, Jina walked alone across the courtyard to Bracken Hall. She knew Lauren, Mary Beth, and Andie were mad at her by the way they'd whispered together all through dinner.

Not that she blamed them. She'd been really mean to them lately. But for some reason, she didn't care. She just wanted to be left alone.

As soon as Jina reached the suite, she grabbed her English lit book and threw herself on her bed. She had so much to do before Saturday's horse show.

Then Jina caught herself.

There was no show for her on Saturday. Superstar was injured. There was no tack to clean, no extra lessons with Todd, no boots to polish. She had all the time in the world to get her homework done.

But she didn't want to study.

She didn't want to do *anything*.

JINA
RIDES TO WIN

by Alison Hart

BULLSEYE BOOKS

Random House 🏠 New York

"You want to have a party tonight?" Jinaki Williams said, staring at her roommates. The four girls were standing in the aisle of Foxhall Academy's newest barn. Superstar, Jina's dapple-gray, hung his head over the bottom of the stall door, munching hay and curiously watching the girls.

Dark-haired Andie Perez nodded. "We've already decided who's getting the chips, the candy, the sodas—"

"And who's coming," Mary Beth Finney chimed in as she brushed her auburn bangs off her forehead.

Lauren Remick counted off the names on her fingers. "My sister Stephanie, Todd, Christina, Ellie—"

"Whoa! Wait a second," Jina interrupted.

"There's no way I can go to a party. I've been up since five o'clock this morning and I spent all day at a horse show. I'm pooped!"

With a sigh, she bent down and began throwing brushes into her tack trunk. She was still dressed in her breeches and riding shirt. Her black boots were propped against her tack trunk.

"Hey, in case you forgot, we were at that show all day, too," Lauren declared, tossing her honey-blond braid behind her shoulder. "We weren't riding like you, but..."

"Besides," Mary Beth added, "you were also the show's Junior Hunter Champion."

"And that deserves a party!" Andie said. She glared at Jina as if daring her to say no.

Jina straightened up again. Lauren, Mary Beth, and Andie were looking at her expectantly.

"Oh, okay. Any excuse for a party, right?" Jina said with a half smile. Actually, she was glad her roommates were so excited about her winning. Since Jina's afternoons and weekends were spent training Superstar and showing, she hadn't had much time to make friends at her new school.

"But first I need to take a shower," Jina said

with a grin at her roommates. Mary Beth's freckled nose was streaked with dirt. Lauren's thick hair had come loose from its braid, and Andie's wild mane was sprinkled with hay.

Mary Beth grinned back. "I think we could *all* use a shower."

With a whoop, Andie turned and raced down the aisle. "First one back to the dorm gets all the hot water!" she called.

With angry squeals, Lauren and Mary Beth ran after her.

Jina watched them leave, then sat wearily on the top of the tack trunk. Maybe her friends were right. Maybe she did need a party.

She and Superstar had won their division championship at the Columbia Show, even though the competition was tough. That meant she was one step closer to winning the Junior Hunter Horse of the Year Award for zone 3. And wasn't that what she'd been working toward ever since February?

She and Superstar had shown hard all last spring, summer, and fall. So far, they'd done great. There were four more shows left before the season ended in November. And Jina was determined to win them all.

A soft nicker interrupted her thoughts, and

Jina turned to Superstar. Her horse bobbed his head and wiggled his lips.

Jina laughed at his comical expression. "I know you're hungry. Dorothy should be along any minute with a big bucket of sweet feed."

She looked down the aisle, wondering if the stable manager had forgotten Superstar. The new ten-stall barn was very quiet.

Foxhall Academy had recently built this barn for students who boarded their own horses at the school. Right now, there were only four horses in the stable.

Jina liked the new barn, with its spacious stalls and the indoor aisle where she could crosstie Superstar. But she missed being with her roommates who rode the Foxhall horses stabled nearby in the older barn.

Jina stood up slowly, stretching out her back muscles with a groan. She still had her tack to put away, boots to polish, breeches to wash—

"There you are," Dorothy said as she came down the aisle. A rubber bucket of grain was banging against her leg. Superstar whinnied excitedly.

Jina laughed. "He sure is happy to see you."

Dorothy plopped the bucket down on the

4

concrete aisle. The stable manager was a stocky woman in her thirties. She wore her hair in a short boyish cut and her blue T-shirt said, "Sell Your Car—Drive a Horse."

"I bet he's not the only one who's hungry." Dorothy studied Jina, hands on her wide hips. "Did you get a chance to eat at the show?"

Jina couldn't remember. "Ummm..."

Dorothy nodded shortly. "That's what I thought. The cafeteria has bag dinners for all you girls coming home late. And you—" she pointed at Jina's chest—"had better get one." Then, opening the stall door, she poured grain into Superstar's feed bucket. He stuck his head in and greedily gulped a mouthful.

Jina leaned on the door and watched as her horse scattered grain everywhere. "You'll remember to take Superstar's sheet off before you turn him out in the morning?" she asked. She nodded to the lightweight cotton blanket he was wearing.

"Yup." Dorothy smacked Superstar affectionately on the shoulder, then shut the stall door. "Now you get out of here, Jina. You're the last rider to leave."

"Okay," Jina agreed. A bag dinner did sound good. Then she'd take a long, hot shower to soothe her sore muscles. And maybe, if she was lucky, her roommates would forget all about the party. Then she could fall into bed and sleep forever.

"Jina, are you in there?" Andie's voice rang through the bathroom door. "If you are, you'd better hurry and get downstairs. We've eaten half the food already. And Todd's here. He wants to play the videotape that he took of the show today." Jina let the hot shower sprinkle on her face. The last thing she wanted to do tonight was watch herself ride on video.

"Jina?" Andie pounded on the door.

Reluctantly, Jina turned off the water. "I'll be out in a second," she called.

"Good. If you're not, we're dragging you down to the party—dressed or not!"

"Great," Jina muttered as she hopped out of the shower. She had no doubt that Andie would carry out her threat.

Wrapping a towel around her, she cracked the door open and peeked into suite 4B. She and her roommates shared one bathroom and one dorm room. Each girl had a single bed, a desk, and a small chest of drawers. One large wardrobe for hanging clothes stood between

Mary Beth's and Lauren's beds. *Whew,* Jina thought. *No one's here. At least I can get dressed in privacy.* Dropping her towel, she rummaged through her drawer for a clean shirt. She was just putting on her jeans when the suite door burst open and her three roommates crowded into the doorway.

"Ready?" Mary Beth, Lauren, and Andie chorused.

"Almost." Quickly, Jina stuck her feet in her moccasins. "You guys look great," she added as she pulled her damp, curly, dark hair back into a short ponytail.

"Lauren here is all spiffed up because she's out to impress Lover-boy Todd," Andie teased.

Jina bit back a grin. She couldn't believe Lauren had a crush on Todd. He had been Jina's trainer for the past two years. Twice a week she and Superstar went to the Middle-field Stables for private lessons. Todd had other students, but so far, Jina had been the most successful on the show circuit.

Lauren flushed. "I am *not* out to impress Todd," she insisted. "I mean, he must be about *twenty.*"

"Oooo. Lauren's in love with an older man," Mary Beth sang out.

Lauren pressed her lips together. "I am not. I just think he's a good rider and—"

"—brave, handsome, dashing." Clasping her hands on her chest, Andie sighed dramatically. Jina and Mary Beth burst out laughing.

"Sometimes you guys act so dumb," Lauren said. "Come on, Jina. Your fans are waiting downstairs."

Abruptly, Jina stopped laughing. "What?"

"Your fans," Lauren repeated. Her smile died when she saw Jina's face.

Fans. The word made Jina's stomach lurch. There was no way she was going to the party if her roommates planned on treating her like some hotshot celebrity.

"I don't have any fans," she said angrily. "And if that's what this party is all about, then I'm not going!"

2

Mary Beth, Lauren, and Andie looked shocked at Jina's outburst.

"Sorry," Jina muttered. Embarrassed, she turned and rummaged through her top drawer, trying to find a necklace she didn't want. *Stupid thing to say, Williams,* Jina told herself angrily. She knew her roommates hadn't really meant *fans.* It wasn't as if people hung around the horse shows asking for autographs.

Andie held up her hands. "Hey, you don't have to bite our heads off. Lauren was just teasing about that fan stuff."

"Honest," Lauren said in a small voice.

"I shouldn't have snapped at you," Jina said. "I was overreacting."

"So, are you coming?" Andie asked, leaning against the doorjamb. She was dressed in tight

9

black jeans and a bright red shirt. Mary Beth and Lauren were already on their way out.

Jina shut the drawer. "Sure," she said, trying to sound extra cheerful.

She followed Andie downstairs. Bracken Hall, the girls' dorm, had a Common Room on the first floor. It could be used by anyone, but during the weekend a small "party" corner could be reserved for special activities.

When Jina and Andie walked into the Common Room, it was already full of girls. They were reading, watching TV, playing cards, and talking. Most of them were Upper School girls. They lived in Bracken Hall, too, but Jina really didn't know them. The oldest students, juniors and seniors, were probably out on dates or weekend passes.

Lauren waved from the back corner where there was a small refrigerator, a microwave, a stereo, and a large-screen TV. A circle of chairs had been pulled up next to the sofa in front of the TV. Todd was kneeling on the floor, fiddling with the VCR.

Mary Beth thrust a bowl in Jina's face as Jina and Andie came over. "Popcorn? Pretzels?"

"I poured you guys some soda," Lauren

said, handing them flowered paper cups.

"Thanks," Jina said. Taking a sip, she looked around. Lauren's older sister, Stephanie, who was a junior at Foxhall, sat on the sofa, talking to Todd. She had long, honey-blond hair like Lauren's, tan legs, and a model's figure.

Next to Stephanie was her roommate, Christina Hernandez. She had been Mary Beth's Big Sister on the first day of school. Jina wondered why Stephanie and Christina were hanging around the Common Room. They usually had dates on Saturday nights.

Over by the food table, Mary Beth was talking to Heidi Olson and Shandra Thomas, two students who were beginning riders like Mary Beth. Behind them, Andie had joined several girls Jina didn't know.

Todd stood up. "Okay, Jina, we're ready."

Reluctantly, Jina moved toward the TV. She was used to going over her riding tapes with Todd to see how she could improve, but not with an audience.

"Hey! That's me!" Lauren exclaimed as she sat on the floor by her sister's feet. On the huge screen, her image was waving at the camera.

"Ooo, my wittle sister is so cute," Stephanie

said, reaching down and pinching Lauren's cheeks.

"And there's Mary Beth," Christina added.

In the video, Mary Beth stood behind Lauren, holding Three Bars Jake, one of the school's horses. Everyone burst out laughing when Jake pulled the lead line from Mary Beth's grasp and walked toward the camera.

On screen, Todd shouted, "Oh no! I'm going to be trampled!" He started to laugh just as Jake's brown muzzle reached up and blotted out the rest of the picture.

Mary Beth pouted. "Hey! I can't help it if Jake's uncontrollable."

"Oh, that Jake's a wild one all right," Andie said, pretending to be serious, and everyone laughed. Jake was a pussycat, but Mary Beth had only been in the Foxhall riding program for three weeks, and she was still afraid of horses. The only one she felt comfortable with was Dangerous Dan, the dead-quiet mount she'd been assigned.

Leaning back against the sofa, Jina relaxed a bit. She hadn't realized that Todd had taken candid shots. Usually he was too busy filming his students. Maybe this would be fun after all.

"So when do we see all the big-deal jumping

stuff?" Stephanie asked, looking at Jina.

"In a minute," Todd said.

A wild mane of hair filled the screen. Andie turned and stuck her tongue out at the video camera as she saddled Superstar. Todd's voice said, "Here's the wonder horse and his amazing groom. Will she get him tacked up in time?"

"Or at least before we fall asleep," Stephanie whispered to Christina. She sounded bored.

"Hey, you don't need to stay," Andie told her. Jina knew that Andie didn't like Stephanie. And she had a good reason, too. The first week at Foxhall, Stephanie had let her sister, Andie, Mary Beth, and Jina take the rap for breaking one of the school's rules.

"I'm sure you two must have hot dates tonight," Mary Beth put in.

Jina clapped a hand over her mouth, stifling a giggle.

Stephanie shrugged. "At least we're old enough to know what a 'hot date' is." She looked straight at Todd, but he didn't seem to notice.

"Would you ladies be quiet," he said. "Jina's riding into the ring now."

Jina turned her attention back to the TV. Superstar was trotting in a circle, getting ready to jump. Head up, ears pricked, he looked every inch a champion.

"Jina, watch how well you approach this first jump," Todd said, not taking his eyes off the TV.

Jina glanced around uneasily. "Uh, Todd, you don't need to comment tonight. I'm sure no one wants to hear—"

"I do!" Lauren exclaimed. "If I'm going to win ribbons like you someday, I want to hear every word."

"Me too," Andie added. "As soon as Magic is better, we're going to start training for the spring shows." Magic was the horse Andie's father had agreed to lease from the school. But because Magic had a detached retina in his eye, he needed an operation and lots of attention before Andie could ever ride him. He was much too wild.

"I wouldn't want to miss this either," a third voice said. Everyone turned around.

A petite, pretty older girl with straight, chin-length blond hair was standing behind the couch with two other girls.

Jina gulped. Ashley Stewart was a junior and one of the best riders at Foxhall. So far, she'd had a good season riding April Fool, the horse she leased from the school. But Jina had beaten her out at the last two shows.

"Hey, Ash," Stephanie said. "Come sit next to me."

"Uh, Steph, I don't think that's such a good idea," Lauren whispered. All the roommates knew how annoyed Ashley was that Jina, a lowly sixth grader, had beaten her out of the last two Junior Hunter Championships.

Ashley waved one hand. "Sorry. We don't nave time. We're meeting our *own* trainers and watching our *own* videos," she said. She turned to her friends. "Right, guys?"

The two girls burst out laughing.

Ashley pretended to be shocked. "You mean we don't *have* our own personal trainers?" she exclaimed in horror. "Well, no wonder we can't beat out Jinaki Williams and her *superstar* horse."

Jina's cheeks burned. She was used to occasional snubs from other riders. But this was different. This was happening at school, where she wanted everyone to like her.

15

"Ashley," Todd said, sounding annoyed, "you're out of line. Why don't you and your friends take off?"

"Yeah. Beat it, Ashley," Andie said. "Go watch that video you made of yourself. You know, 'Dracula Meets Witch Woman.'"

A couple of girls twittered. Ashley raised one brow, and looked down at Jina, her arms crossed.

"So, Williams, do you pay your trainer and your groom to speak for you?"

Jina jumped up. "Andie's not my groom," she said. "She helps me at the shows just like Missy helps you—because Mrs. Caufield assigned her."

Ashley snorted. "A kid like you who's rich enough to pay such big bucks for her horse must have her own groom."

Jina stepped around the sofa. *It's not fair,* she thought. Ashley was making her look like a rich, spoiled snob in front of her friends.

"It just explains why you're winning," Ashley went on, leaning toward Jina. "*Anyone* could win shows riding a fifty-thousand-dollar horse. Even you!"

3

Jina was so angry, she couldn't speak.

She reached out and shoved the blond girl in the chest.

Ashley stumbled backward into the table of snacks. With a startled cry, she lost her balance and fell into the bowl of potato chips.

Andie choked back a laugh, and Lauren's and Mary Beth's mouths dropped open. Stephanie and Christina jumped up from the sofa to help their friend up.

Ashley's face was red with anger. But Jina was furious, too. She'd worked too hard and too long for somebody to tell her that she'd only won because of the price tag on her horse.

"I deserve every ribbon I win," Jina told Ashley between clenched teeth.

The older girl angrily yanked her arms from her friends' grasps. Then she took a deep breath and composed her face into a smooth mask.

"Maybe," she said coolly. "But there are a lot of shows before the season ends. And I predict *you* won't be the final winner."

With that, she spun around and strode across the Common Room just as Ms. Shiroo, the dorm mother, came in through the door with another student. Frowning, she looked at Ashley's departing group, then back at Jina and her friends in the corner.

Uh-oh, Jina thought. *Someone told Shiroo there was trouble.*

Ms. Shiroo talked a minute with Ashley and her friends. It seemed as though the older girls were telling the dorm mother that there was no problem. "Hey, don't worry," Andie said, touching Jina on the arm. "Everyone knows Ashley's a jerk. Even Ms. Shiroo."

When Ms. Shiroo looked back one more time at Jina and left, Jina breathed a sigh of relief.

She turned to face her friends. They were eating chips and drinking their sodas, pretending that nothing had happened. Even Andie

18

seemed extremely busy now chowing down popcorn.

But Jina knew what her roomates were really thinking.

This past week at Foxhall, she'd almost started to feel that she fit in. But now, thanks to Ashley, everyone would probably go back to thinking of her as that rich snob with the expensive horse.

Jina looked down at her hands. They were still balled into fists.

"Hey, Jina, come watch the rest of the video," Lauren suggested finally.

"No thanks. I'm really tired," Jina said, blinking fast to hold back tears. "I think I'll go to bed."

Todd nodded. "We can look at this later," he said, ejecting the video. "And hey, don't let Ashley get to you."

Jina gave him a small smile. Todd was used to girls like Ashley. He'd shown in the A-rated circuit since he was a little kid, so he knew how other riders could react when the competition got tough. And at Middlefield Stables, where he worked, fifty-thousand-dollar horses weren't unusual.

"Jina! Jina Williams!" a voice rang out

across the Common Room. "Phone call on the fourth floor!"

Saved, Jina thought. She forced a brief smile. "Got to go. Thanks for the party, guys." Then she took off for the stairs.

"Jina! Sweetheart!" It was her mother on the other line. "How'd the show go?"

"Great." Jina felt better now that she heard her mother's voice. "Superstar and I won the Junior Hunter Championship. That means we're definitely on our way to the Horse of the Year Award!"

Her mother shrieked, "Yahoo! I knew my baby could do it. Guess what?"

"What?" Jina asked, crossing her fingers. Maybe her mom had finally gotten some time off so they could spend an afternoon together. Just the two of them.

"I'm coming to see you ride in Saturday's show. Isn't that terrific?"

Jina was horrified.

"You're coming to the show?" she repeated. That was the last thing she wanted! Now *everybody* would know about her mom. "Can't we just get together for dinner or something? We haven't been able to just sit and talk for—"

"I know, baby, I know," said her mother,

soothingly. "There will be plenty of time for that later. But the show's right outside of Baltimore so it'll be easy for me to get to. Jamison's already put it in the schedule."

"But—"

"No *buts*. You just work hard this week. I want to watch you win another championship!" Her mom made kissing noises into the phone, then said good-bye.

Jina hung up, her eyes filling with tears.

Why was her mother coming to the show?

It would only make things worse.

"I love Sundays," Lauren said happily the next morning. She lay back on a towel she'd spread on the school's courtyard lawn. "Especially when it's so sunny and warm."

Beside her, Andie grunted in agreement. She wore a bathing suit top and shorts. Holding a reflector under her neck, she directed the sun's rays on her dark face.

Jina and Mary Beth were sharing a towel. Mary Beth had slathered her nose with zinc oxide. Now she was busily rubbing sunblock on her freckled arms. Jina was trying to read her history text, but it was hard to concentrate on studying outdoors.

The courtyard was crowded with girls. Most were sunbathing in the last of the warm September sun. Others threw Frisbees, jogged along the sidewalks, or visited with friends.

"I hate Sundays," Mary Beth said as she put on her Orioles baseball cap. "It means there's only one more day until Monday. And *that* means the beginning of endless homework."

"Speaking of homework," Jina said, "am I the only one who has to study?"

"Yup," the others answered.

"We got ours done Friday night while you were braiding Superstar for the show," Mary Beth said.

"Andie even did hers. Kind of a miracle, don't you think?" Lauren giggled.

Andie snorted. "I wasn't the one who spent the whole night moaning over math."

Ignoring her, Lauren reached into her backpack and pulled out a bottle of nail polish.

"Want to do your nails?" she asked Mary Beth and Jina.

"Sure," Jina said, putting down her history book. She wasn't getting any reading done anyway.

Lauren passed her the bottle. "So Jina, did Superstar really cost that much money?"

Jina flushed. *Oh great*, she thought. *Here come the questions*. Hunching over, she busily brushed pink pearl polish on her toes, pretending not to hear Lauren.

Mary Beth whistled. "Fifty thousand dollars!" she said. "That's more than my parents paid for our house!"

Jina shrugged. "Well, really good show horses are expensive."

"I'll say," Andie said. "Your mom must make big bucks." She lowered the reflector. "What does she do, anyway, make counterfeit money?"

Lauren and Mary Beth laughed. Then Lauren snapped her fingers. "I've got it," Lauren said. "I bet she's a movie star. Right Jina?"

"Wrong." Jina jumped up, almost knocking over the bottle of polish. "She's just my mother. So lay off the stupid questions— okay?"

Without waiting for an answer, she grabbed her textbook and raced off.

23

"You did it again, Williams," Jina muttered as she reached the shadows of the tall oak trees that lined the courtyard. "You lost your cool."

She swung open Bracken Hall's heavy door and went inside. The building was quiet. Everyone was outside.

Slowly, Jina climbed to the fourth floor, her feet dragging. It didn't seem fair that she still had homework. She even had a history report due Friday on the American Revolution.

Jina had chosen the topic "Blacks in the Revolutionary War." So far, she hadn't found much in the encyclopedias. Why hadn't she picked an easy topic like "The Boston Tea Party"?

Party. Jina sighed. What a fiasco that had been. Ashley and her big mouth.

But what really bothered her was the way her roommates were acting now—asking how much her horse cost and what her mother did. She should have expected it. That's what had happened at her last school.

And now it was happening again.

"Magic's operation is next Thursday," Andie told the roommates worriedly as the girls walked up the hill toward the stables.

The girls were wearing their riding clothes and carrying their helmets. The day's classes were over and it was time for the riding program.

Andie sighed. "I hope it goes okay," she said.

"I thought you told us the operation was next Friday," Lauren said.

Andie nodded. "It was, but the vet had a cancellation. Mrs. Caufield just told me at lunch. They vanned Magic to Dr. Holden's office this afternoon. He does the surgery there."

As they approached the stables, Jina listened to Andie with only half an ear. Her mind was whirling about what to do with Superstar. His regime this week had to be perfect to get him in peak mental and physical condition for the Auburn show.

Todd had said to give the horse a break—a leisurely jog on a trail. That sounded like fun to Jina.

And she needed fun. Maybe she'd ask Lauren or Andie to go with her. School rules required students to trail ride with a buddy.

Jina turned her attention back to her roommates.

"So what will the vet do to Magic?" Mary Beth was asking.

"I'm not sure," Andie replied. "Mrs. Caufield said they'll operate using laser beams, just like they do on people."

"How long will Magic be laid up after the operation?" Lauren asked.

Andie looked glum.

"He'll be back at Foxhall on Thursday. But I won't be able to ride him for about three weeks."

Three weeks? Jina didn't know how Andie could wait that long. "What will you do until then?" she asked.

"Caufield's letting me ride Ranger again." Andie grinned. "I'm kind of excited."

Mary Beth sighed. "At least you can ride by yourself," she said. "Sometimes I wonder if I'll ever get off the lead line."

"Don't get discouraged," Lauren said. "It's only your third week. And your posting looks pretty good."

"Yeah, but every time Mrs. Caufield talks about unhooking the longe line, I panic. What if Dan runs away with me?"

The four girls stopped in the stable's courtyard. The horseshoe-shaped barn was busy with riders tacking up and grooming horses.

"Hey Andie and Lauren, do either of you want to go on a trail ride with me?" Jina asked.

Andie shook her head. "Sorry. It's been a while since I've ridden, so Caufield wants me to work in the ring."

"And Whisper and I are practicing our collected trot," Lauren said. "The dressage competition is only two weeks away!"

"Oh." Jina looked down at her paddock boots. *They're just making excuses,* she thought. *They probably don't want to go with me.*

"Well, we'd better get moving," Mary Beth said. "Mrs. Caufield likes everyone in the ring on time." With a wave, she, Andie, and Lauren headed toward the tack room to get their grooming kits.

Jina watched them go. Then she slowly headed toward the new barn, where Superstar was waiting for her. Walking down the spotlessly clean aisle, she grabbed his leather halter from the hook by his stall. Since it was a sunny day, Superstar would probably be grazing in his private paddock out back. Unlike most of the school horses, Superstar could never be turned out with another horse. There was too much risk of an injury from a playful kick or bite.

Jina whistled as she rounded the corner of the building. Lifting his head, the gray nickered and trotted over to the gate. His dappled coat gleamed and his muscles rippled.

Jina gazed at her horse in admiration. He was so beautiful! Leaning over the gate, she stroked his nose. So what if he'd cost fifty thousand dollars? Two years ago, when she'd first seen Superstar, she'd known he was the horse for her.

"Are you lonely out here all by yourself?" she asked, as she unlatched the gate. The horse pushed her with his nose in reply.

Jina slipped the halter over his muzzle and

buckled the cheek strap. Then she led him into the stable, halting him in the aisle. After snapping the crossties onto both side rings of his halter, she bent to get a brush from her grooming kit.

Twenty minutes later, Superstar was clean and tacked up. Jina shoved her helmet on her head and walked the gray outside. The two outdoor rings were busy with riders taking lessons.

"Maybe we'll just walk around," Jina told Superstar as she gathered the reins in her left hand. "That'll be giving you a break like Todd said."

Sticking her left toe in the stirrup, Jina hopped twice on her right leg and jumped into the saddle. Superstar stood motionless, his ears pricked as he watched the horses trotting and cantering around the closest ring. But when Jina touched him lightly with her calves, he immediately moved off in a smooth walk.

Leaving the reins loose, Jina walked Superstar down the gravel drive to the lower ring and around the split rail fence, letting him look at everything. Then she halted him by the gate.

In the middle of the ring, Mary Beth was jogging Dangerous Dan around a small circle.

Despite his name, the big draft horse cross was gentle and used to beginners. A longe line was attached to his bridle. Dorothy was holding the other end and hollering instructions.

Jina grinned. Mary Beth's face was bright red, and sweat trickled down her cheeks. She made posting look like torture, but Jina had to admit she was a lot smoother than last week.

At the far end of the ring, Katherine Parks, the dressage instructor, worked with Lauren and three other girls on the collected trot.

Lauren and Whisper looked the best. Whisper was the chestnut school horse Lauren had been assigned. The horse was small, but she had a long stride and smooth way of moving that made her stand out. And petite Lauren, who had a natural seat on a horse, fit her mount perfectly.

Jina knew Lauren was excited about the upcoming dressage competition. In dressage, riders took their horses in a solo test around a rectangular arena. Horse and rider had to halt, walk, trot, and canter in a series of movements while the judge scored them.

A warm breeze brushed Jina's cheek. Propping one hand on Superstar's rump, she leaned back in the saddle and raised her face to the sun. It felt good just to watch everyone else for once.

"Taking a vacation?" a voice asked.

Jina twisted around in her saddle. Ashley was mounted behind her on April Fool. Impatiently, the mare pawed the ground and swished her tail. From the dark gleam on April's neck, Jina could tell she'd just finished a workout.

"S-sort of," Jina stammered. Ashley always made her nervous.

Making a tsk-tsking sound, Ashley shook her head. "Bad idea if you ask me. Auburn is going to be one tough show." She narrowed her eyes and gave Jina a superior look. "That means only the toughest rider is going to win," she threw over her shoulder as she turned April toward the barn.

When Ashley had gone, Jina realized how tight her fingers were grasping the reins. She took a deep breath and reached down to pat Superstar's neck.

"Ashley's right," she told him. "Auburn *is* going to be one tough show. We'd better get to work—because there's no way I'm going to let Ashley Stewart win!"

5

"It's going to be a *lousy* horse show, Mom," Jina said into the phone. "Really."

It was right after dinner, and she'd called her mother at home from the pay phone in the Common Room. "I've competed at Auburn before, remember? It's crowded, hot, dusty—"

"That's fine with me, baby."

Jina sighed. When her mom made up her mind, she never changed it. "'Bye, Mom," she said. "See you Saturday."

"Hey, that's great. Your mom's coming to the show?" someone asked.

Startled, Jina spun around and saw Lauren standing behind her.

Jina groaned silently. She'd snuck down to the Common Room before study time so no one would hear her conversation.

Lauren's blue eyes twinkled. "I can't wait to meet your mysterious mom. Andie thinks you don't talk about her because she's in prison."

"Prison?" Jina repeated in disbelief.

"Then why the big secret?" Lauren asked. She followed Jina out of the Common Room and up the steps.

"There's no big secret," Jina said, hoping she sounded convincing. "I just don't want my mom to come to my show because she...she makes me nervous." That was true. It just wasn't the whole truth.

Lauren nodded. "I understand," she said as they continued up the steps to the fourth floor. "My first dressage competition is in two weeks and I've already got butterflies. You know," she added casually, "I'd love to watch one of your lessons at Middlefield Stables sometime."

Jina raised one brow. "This wouldn't have anything to do with Todd, would it?"

"Of course not!" Lauren protested, blushing. "I think you're one of the best riders at Foxhall. I figure just watching one of your lessons would teach me tons."

Jina pressed her lips together. Lauren sounded very sincere. "Maybe Mrs. Caufield will give you permission to come with me some afternoon when it's raining. Middlefield's indoor riding arena is pretty neat. It's so huge they can fit an entire jump course in it."

Suddenly, the suite door flew open. "Hey, you guys, get in here," Andie said. The lights inside the suite were out, except for a small horseshoe-shaped night-light, and Mary Beth was on the bed by the window. Her nose was plastered against the glass.

"What's going on?" Lauren asked as Andie shut the door and pushed them toward the window.

"Another ghost?" Jina guessed. The first week of school, Mary Beth thought she saw a ghost floating across the courtyard. It turned out to be a sleepwalking student.

"Even better," Mary Beth whispered. "It's snotty old Ashley—with a *guy!*"

"What!" Jina and Lauren chorused, crowding next to Mary Beth.

The courtyard lights were on, and Jina could just make out two figures standing on the walk in front of the dorm. One was definitely Ashley. Even in the dim light, her straight blond hair shimmered.

But who was the guy?

She caught her breath the same second

Lauren cried out, "She's talking to *Todd*!"

"Todd?" Andie echoed, pushing closer. "What's he doing here?"

"He has special permission to see me during study hours," Jina said, frowning. "To show me training videos and stuff. But why is he talking to *her*?"

"Maybe he likes her?" Andie said.

"It's not like he's her boyfriend or anything," Lauren snapped. She ran over and threw herself face down on the ruffly pink bed.

"Uh-oh," Andie said under her breath. Jina and Mary Beth looked over at Lauren, then out the window again. Todd was walking toward the dorm, but Ashley had disappeared.

"I bet Ashley's pumping him for information about the show on Saturday," Jina said, almost to herself. "You know, anything she can use to win." She bit her lip nervously. "I hope he doesn't tell her anything."

"So ask him," Andie advised.

"I guess." Jina sighed. Then she looked over at Lauren. Her roommate had picked up a book and was pretending to read it. Lauren probably felt hurt even though her crush on Todd was kind of silly. But she didn't want to embarrass Lauren by saying anything.

"I'm going downstairs," Jina said finally.

She found Todd in the Common Room over by the VCR. Ashley was nowhere in sight.

Should she ask him why he'd been talking to her chief competition?

No, she decided quickly as Todd turned and waved her over. It would sound so stupid. Ashley was just a flirt. And Todd would know she'd been spying on him.

Jina plastered a smile on her face. It didn't matter what Todd told Ashley. It didn't even matter if her mother came to the show.

She was going to win—no matter what.

"Keep your fingers crossed, guys!" Andie hollered to the roommates on Tuesday morning.

Jina was still in bed, trying to get an extra minute of sleep. She opened one eye to see Andie standing in the bathroom doorway. Andie was yelling to them as she dried her hair.

"What did you say, Andie?" Mary Beth yelled back. She was sitting on her bed, pulling on a pair of tan jeans.

"KEEP YOUR FINGERS CROSSED!"

Andie screamed. "MAGIC'S OPERATION IS IN TWO DAYS!"

"OH!" Mary Beth nodded.

"WOULD YOU GUYS SHUT UP!" Lauren yelled from her desk chair. She'd been furiously writing and erasing for the last fifteen minutes. "I HAVE TO FINISH THIS MATH!"

Jina rolled over in bed and stuck the pillow over her head. What a crazy zoo their suite was—every single morning!

Andie switched off the dryer. "What?"

Mary Beth hopped over to the window, still trying to zip her tight jeans. "Oh no, it's raining."

"Great! That means riding in the indoor arena, if we're lucky," Andie said. She came up beside Mary Beth. "Or else it means cleaning tack and listening to a lecture on hoof rot."

"Hoof rot? Euw." Mary Beth shuddered and wrinkled her freckled nose.

Jina threw back her quilt. "Hey, Lauren, maybe you can go to Middlefield Stables with me today. It would be nice to have some company for once."

"That'd be great." Lauren said without

looking up from her paper. "I'll ask Caufield after Morning Meeting."

"Morning Meeting!" Mary Beth and Andie chorused.

"Yeah, guys. Every Tuesday, remember?" Lauren closed her textbook and tucked it into her backpack. "You'd better hurry, Jina."

Half an hour later, the roommates were seated in the second row of the auditorium behind the administration building. The large room was filled with girls wearing raincoats and carrying soggy backpacks.

Next to Jina, Lauren was turned in her seat, waving at Stephanie. On the other side of Lauren, Andie was arguing with Mary Beth about who the cutest teacher was—Mr. Lyons, the gym teacher, or Mr. Vassalotti, who taught advanced math to the juniors and seniors.

A buzz of conversation echoed around the room until Mr. Frawley, the headmaster of Foxhall Academy, tapped on the microphone. As usual, he was the only faculty member dressed in a white shirt, suit, and tie. Half glasses were perched on his nose.

"Good morning, Foxhall girls," he greeted them. "We have a lot of things to tell you today—announcements, activity dates, games, and meeting times. But first I'd like to recognize some of our students."

"Millie Lacey—" The headmaster looked around the audience and an older student raised her hand. "Congratulations on winning our Gold Key Award, Millie. This award is presented each month to an outstanding Foxhall senior who has demonstrated her commitment to Foxhall and its standards."

"They should call it the Most Boring Student Award," Jina heard Andie mutter.

"Thank you, Millie," Mr. Frawley continued. "And now I'd like to recognize one of our new students, a sixth grader."

Jina looked over her shoulder at the rest of her class, trying to figure out which girl Mr. Frawley was talking about. Andie, Mary Beth, and Lauren craned their necks, too.

"She's the first Foxhall student to make the front page of the *Woodville Gazette* for this school year, and we're very proud of her,"

Reaching back, Mr. Frawley picked up a folded newspaper from the stage. When he opened it, Jina's eyes widened in horror. She could just make out a huge photo of her jumping Superstar!

The headmaster was talking about *her*!

6

Jina felt the color drain from her face. She couldn't believe it! Not only was her picture in the paper, but Mr. Frawley was announcing it to the whole world!

"Foxhall Girl Wins Championship," the headmaster read the headline aloud. "And the article begins—Jinaki Williams, a sixth-grade student at Foxhall Academy, has racked up her tenth championship for the season. Will she win the Junior Hunter Horse of the Year Award?"

Mr. Frawley read on and on. Finally, he stopped and looked around the auditorium. "Jinaki, please stand up so we can all congratulate you."

Jina froze. There was no way she was going to stand up. It would be much too embarrassing. Already she could hear whispers around her—probably Ashley and her friends snickering that Jina Williams had only won because she had a private trainer and a fifty-thousand-dollar horse.

"Hey, Jina." Lauren's elbow dug into her side. "Stand up."

Jina looked at her blankly. "Stand *up*, Williams," Andie's insistent voice came from the other side.

Slowly, stiffly, Jina half-stood. She felt all eyes were looking at her, and then the applause broke out.

"Congratulations, Jina," Mr. Frawley said into the microphone, but Jina had already sunk back into her seat and buried her head in her hands. Now Ashley and her friends would hate her more than ever.

When Morning Meeting was finally over, the troops of girls filed noisily from the auditorium. Jina stared straight ahead, not looking at anyone.

"Wow, can you believe you made the front page of the paper, Jina?" Lauren said. "I would have died."

"Jina almost did, too," Andie said. "What was wrong with you in there, Williams?

Why were you acting so weird and nervous?"

Jina dropped her gaze. "I didn't think Frawley needed to tell the whole school, that's all."

"Why not?" Mary Beth asked as they stopped in front of the bulletin board. "Aren't you proud of yourself and Superstar?"

Jina nodded. "Sure. But that picture in the paper and all that congratulations stuff make everything seem like such a big deal."

"Oh, I get it." Andie nodded knowingly. "You don't want the other riders to think you're rubbing it in. Hey, it serves Ashley right."

Jina let out an exasperated sigh. "Can we just drop it?"

"And then your name was called again," Mary Beth persisted. "Why does Ms. Thaney want to see you?"

"Lots of other girls' names were called. Besides, Ms. Thaney is my adviser," Jina said.

"And our history teacher," Lauren reminded her. "You didn't flunk something, did you?"

"Oooo." Andie's dark eyes gleamed. "Don't tell me Miss Made-the-Headlines got in trouble."

"No," Jina snapped. "And don't call me that."

"Well, it must be something important," Mary Beth pointed out. "No other sixth graders got called."

Jina gritted her teeth. Why couldn't her roommates just leave her alone? "What does it matter to you guys, anyway? Andie sees Dean Wilkes every day, and you're not asking *her* a million questions."

"That's 'cause we know how Andie messed up," Lauren said, giggling.

Andie planted her hands on her hips. "Hey, I've been real good lately. I have to be if my dad's going to let me keep Magic."

"Oh yeah?" Mary Beth said. "What about those water balloons that mysteriously exploded on the courtyard yesterday?"

Andie shrugged. "Well, I've been *pretty* good."

"Ms. Thaney wants to see me right now," Jina said, turning down the hall. "I'll see you guys in English second period, okay?"

"We want to know *everything*," Lauren called after her.

Jina rolled her eyes. As though she could ever forget it!

The hall that led to Old House, the administration building, was crowded with girls carrying backpacks. The tile floor was slick with wet footprints, and the walls of the old building smelled musty.

Jina climbed the stairs to the second floor where the teachers' offices were located. All the faculty at Foxhall acted as student advisers. Jina had already met with Ms. Thaney, whom she liked very much, several times. But this was the first time she'd been summoned for a special appointment.

Ms. Thaney had a small cubicle in a room labeled "History Department." Jina peered in the doorway. Seated at a desk behind a partition, her adviser was grading papers.

"Jina, I'm so glad you came right up." Ms. Thaney was youngish. Today she wore black stirrup pants, a long knit top, and dangly earrings. She was an enthusiastic teacher and made history sort of fun.

"Sit down," she said, waving at a straight-backed chair against the wall.

Hesitantly, Jina perched on the edge. "You wanted to see me?"

Ms. Thaney nodded briskly as she riffled through the papers on her desk. "First I wanted to congratulate you on your win Saturday. The whole school's talking about it!"

44

Great. "Thank you," Jina said.

"And I'm very excited about the title of your upcoming report for class, "Blacks in the Revolutionary War," she went on. "But I don't have the initial outline that was due last Friday."

Jina sucked in her breath. "Outline? I, um, must have forgotten all about it."

Ms. Thaney smiled. "Don't panic. Sometimes it's hard for sixth graders to keep everything straight. And you've got a lot going on for someone who's only eleven."

"I'll be twelve soon," Jina said.

"That's right. You have a birthday next week, don't you?" Ms. Thaney sat back in her chair. "Still, Mrs. Caufield and I want to make sure you're able to handle all of your responsibilities. Foxhall has many talented students who excel in sports and the arts. Our job is to see that they're able to keep up academically as well."

Jina clenched her fingers together. "Oh, that's never been a problem. At my other school, I got straight A's. I was showing then too."

"I know." Ms. Thaney smiled again. "You're an exceptional girl, Jina, and we're proud to have you at Foxhall. Just remember, we're here if you need us. And don't take on too much!"

"Keep him steady, keep him steady," Todd called from the center of Middlefield's huge indoor arena. "Sink your weight in your heels. Loosen up. Pretend you're approaching the jump and *ten* judges are watching you and Superstar. You want each of them to give you a perfect score."

Perfect score, Jina repeated to herself as she and Superstar cantered down the side of the indoor ring. *Weight in the heels. Loosen up. Steady.*

Boom! Thunder suddenly crashed overhead, echoing through the big steel building. Superstar's ears flicked back and forth. Jina could feel his muscles tense slightly.

Rat-a-tat. Rat-a-tat. Like a noisy drum, rain started to beat on the metal roof. Then it began to pour, sounding like thousands of blasting machine guns.

"Easy, Superstar," Jina soothed. She could no longer hear Todd. But it didn't matter. For their lesson today, they were only jumping one fence—but it had to be *perfect*. She had to block out everything else.

Jina took a deep breath. Gradually, the sound of the thunder and heavy rain disappeared. All she heard now was the rhythmic *da-da-dump* of Superstar's hooves on the tanbark. And all she could feel was the cool air blowing across her cheeks as they approached the jump, their bodies moving as one. Three strides away, Jina deepened her seat. Superstar shortened his stride slightly, meeting the jump at just the right spot. Folding his forelegs to his chest, he propelled himself into the air. With rounded back and arched neck, he sailed over the fence as if he had wings.

Grinning to herself, Jina let the gray canter in a small circle. It had felt so good! Like Pegasus flying to the heavens.

Someone started clapping. Jina looked over to see Lauren sitting in the bleachers. She was applauding so loudly, Jina could even hear her over the beating rain.

Jina settled deep in the saddle. She pulled Superstar to a trot, then a walk. He shook his head as if to say—"Is that all?" Then the horse relaxed and strode over to the bleachers.

Lauren was saying something to Todd. Her roommate was leaning over the partition that separated the seats from the ring, gazing at Todd as if he were a famous rock star.

"That was it," Todd said when Jina rode close enough to hear him. "The perfect jump. If you do all your fences like that at Auburn, you'll win your third championship in a row, no contest."

"Yeah!" Lauren bounced up and down like a cheerleader. Jina started to laugh, until she noticed the serious expression on Todd's face.

"I've been debating with myself all week whether I should tell you this, Jina," he said finally.

Jina's heart skipped a beat. "What?"

"I was afraid you might get too excited."

"Tell me what?" Jina's voice rose.

Todd took a deep breath. "If you win the championship at Saturday's show, Jina Williams—" he paused and his mouth broke into a huge grin—"you'll have enough points to win the Horse of the Year Award!"

7

Jina caught her breath. If she won Saturday, it would all be over! She could relax and—

But what if she *didn't* win?

"Jina, aren't you excited?" Lauren said.

"I guess so," Jina replied.

Todd frowned. "I shouldn't have told you. Now you're going to worry yourself sick."

Jina shook her head. "No. I'm glad you told me." Dropping the reins, she slid off Superstar as another burst of thunder rumbled through the arena.

"Even if you don't win at Auburn, you can still win the Horse of the Year Award," Todd said. "It would mean three more tough shows this season. If you win Saturday, you can relax."

"Wait until I tell Andie and Mary Beth!" Lauren said eagerly.

Jina spun around. "Don't you dare!" she warned. "I don't need them bugging me about winning, too."

Lauren's face fell. "Am *I* bugging you?"

"I didn't mean you," Jina said quickly. "I meant, uh—Todd," she said, glancing at her trainer.

He grinned. "I'll take that as a compliment. After all, bugging you is my job."

Jina grinned back. But inside, she was beginning to get very, very nervous.

"So do you think Todd likes me, Jina?" Lauren asked as the girls walked through the rain on their way to the library. It was Thursday night, and the four roommates had permission to spend their study time researching their history projects.

Jina hunched lower under Lauren's umbrella. *What a lousy question*, she thought. *No matter how I answer, Lauren will get upset.*

"Who cares about Todd," Andie cut in. She was walking under another umbrella with Mary Beth. "Let's talk about Magic. Did I tell you his operation went great?"

"Three times at dinner," Mary Beth grumbled. "You gave us all the gross details about how the veterinarian blasted laser beams into Magic's eyeball."

It had been raining for three days. Foxhall's indoor ring was too small for all the girls in the riding program, so the last two afternoons had been spent watching slides, lectures, and demonstrations. Only the students getting ready for Saturday's show had been allowed to ride. But the weather was so cold and damp, neither Jina nor Superstar had enjoyed their workouts.

"The operation was *not* gross," Andie said indignantly. She cocked her head. "Maybe I'll be a vet when I grow up."

Mary Beth snickered. "When will that be?"

"Hey, I don't need any jokes from someone carrying a Cinderella umbrella," Andie shot back.

"Will you two *children* shut up," Lauren said. She stopped so suddenly on the library steps that her umbrella poked Jina in the forehead.

"Yes, mother," Mary Beth and Andie chorused.

Jina opened the library's heavy wooden

door, and the four girls rushed into the foyer out of the rain. The marble floor was dotted with dripping umbrellas.

"So, Jina, are you going to answer my question?" Lauren asked. "Do you think Todd likes me? I mean, just a little?"

Three pairs of eyes looked expectantly at Jina.

She fiddled nervously with her raincoat buttons, trying to find the right thing to say.

"Uh, I think—" she stammered.

"She thinks Todd's too old for you," Andie said, flipping off the hood of her yellow slicker. "Besides, he's probably dated a hundred girls. And your big experience was the sixth-grade dance, remember?"

"A hundred girls?" Lauren squeaked.

Andie nodded. "At least. Right Jina?"

Jina shrugged. "I don't know. But he's really busy riding and teaching lessons. He may not have that much time to date."

"Oh." Lauren's mouth drooped as she set her umbrella on the floor to dry. Then she brightened. "I guess that's better than finding out he has a girlfriend."

"Right," Jina agreed quickly. "Now I've got to get to work. I owe Ms. Thaney that history outline and the opening paragraph of my report."

"You're kidding. *You* didn't hand in the outline yet?" Andie whispered as they trooped down the aisle to the reference room. The library had huge cathedral ceilings and every word echoed through it.

"No," Jina said. She waited for Andie to make some snide comment.

But Andie just grinned. "Cool. Maybe you'll end up with a homework chart like me."

When they reached the reference room, Jina followed her roommates to a long wooden table. Several other girls from her history class were already there, working.

Jina flung her backpack on the table, took off her raincoat, and went to the card catalog. She couldn't believe how far behind she was with this stupid report.

With a sigh, she slammed shut the drawer of subject cards. Nothing under "Blacks and War." She'd have to ask the media specialist for help.

"Blacks in the Revolutionary War?" Mr. Chan said. He smiled and pointed to a corner shelf. "I know just the book."

Thank goodness, Jina thought. A few

moments later, she was back at the table reading.

"Don't forget, we have to use at least three different sources," Mary Beth whispered from behind a stack of books.

"I know," Jina whispered back. "But I can't find three different sources. What am I supposed to do, make them up?"

"Sure," Andie replied, leaning across the table. "I'd be glad to help."

Jina gave her a disgusted look. She'd never cheated in her life.

On the other hand...

Her head began to pound. She had a book to finish reading for literature, she had to clean her tack and boots, and her mother was coming to Saturday's show.

Jina looked over at her roommates. Ever since Sunday, no one had mentioned her mother. But once they met her—

Jina rubbed her forehead. She couldn't think about that now.

When Lauren and Mary Beth left the table to get more books, Jina leaned toward Andie.

"Okay, Andie," she whispered, glancing nervously over her shoulder. "Help me fake those two sources."

8

"Where's my girth?" Jina asked Andie, looking around frantically. It was Saturday morning, and there were only five minutes left before her first class.

"Attached to your saddle," Andie said. She was bent over, brushing hoof polish on Superstar's left rear hoof.

"No, it's not," Jina replied, her voice rising. The announcer had just called the Junior Hunter Warm-up Class at the Auburn Horse Show.

Jina was ready to go. Her hair was tucked neatly under her riding helmet. Her black, pinstriped hunt coat hugged her frame neatly, and her white shirt and breeches were pressed and spotless. She'd buffed her tall black boots until they glistened, and the white silk choker around her neck was secured with a sparkling diamond-studded pin.

Andie looked up. She had polish on her nose and cheeks. "Well, that's where I put it."

Jina swung the saddle around, showing Andie the empty girth straps on the right side. "Then where is it?" she asked.

Andie jumped up. "Okay. Hold your horses. Maybe it's in the back of Dorothy's truck." Handing Superstar's reins to Jina, Andie ran to look.

Jina couldn't believe her rotten luck. Auburn was one of the biggest shows of the season. And if she did well, she could sew up the Horse of the Year Award. But her mother was coming, they'd called her class, and now her girth was missing!

What next? she muttered to herself as she threw the saddle pad and saddle on Superstar's back. Carefully, she smoothed and adjusted the pad, then checked him over. His braids were perfect, nostrils clean, hooves polished, tail—

"It's not there," Andie announced as she came around the end of the van.

Jina stopped dead. "What?"

"Class three, Junior Hunter Warm-up, is

56

now proceeding in ring B," the announcer blasted over the loud speaker. "First rider—"

"Oh great!" Jina snapped. "I'm jumping fourth. I've *got* to find that girth."

Andie raised one palm. "Don't panic. Go on down to the warm-up ring. I'll find a girth."

"I need *my* girth," Jina wailed, but Andie had already disappeared around the van again.

Trying to stay calm, Jina led Superstar slowly down the gravel drive, passing a long row of horse vans and trailers. The Auburn show grounds were crowded with spectators walking around with programs and riders grooming their horses.

When she reached the warm-up ring, Jina groaned. The ground was chopped and muddy, after four days of rain.

Pulling out a rag that she'd tucked in her waistband, Jina wiped her already splattered boots. Mud stained her black gloves.

She glanced anxiously around for Andie. Her roommate was running down the drive, a girth flapping in her arms.

"Whose is that?" Jina asked.

"Who cares?" Andie panted as she buckled the girth on the right side. "It's clean and I think it's the right length."

"It *better* be the right length," Jina said. "George Monroe, the judge, looks at all those little details. I can't *believe* you lost my girth." She reached under Superstar's belly and grabbed the buckled end.

"And I can't *believe* you're giving me such a hard time," Andie retorted, glaring at Jina across the saddle. "Especially since *I didn't lose it!*"

Jina yanked up on the straps. "Okay, okay. Maybe you didn't lose it. And it looks like this one should work. Thanks." Quickly, she finished buckling the girth.

Forget it, she told herself. *Breathe deep. Get yourself under control.*

Without looking back at Andie, Jina pulled down the stirrup, mounted Superstar, and squeezed him into a trot. She could see Todd standing by the entry gate of ring B, peering over the crowd for her. She and Superstar would just have enough time for two circles around the warm-up ring. Then they'd be on deck. Thank goodness the warm-up class didn't count toward the championship.

"Are you all right?" Todd asked when Jina finally jogged to the entry gate. Pulling a rag from his waistband, he briskly wiped off

Superstar's legs. "I thought you were lost or something."

"I'm fine," she said, looking around for her mother. It didn't look as though she'd arrived yet.

"Number thirty-nine," the announcer called. Todd gave Jina one last swift check, then sent her into the ring with a nod.

She took a deep breath as she circled Superstar. *Just one perfect jump*, she told herself as she steered the dapple-gray toward the first fence. *Then another and another*, she repeated as Superstar flew over the course of eight jumps. He finished with a smooth leap over the crossbar.

"You did it!" Todd beamed as Jina and Superstar walked through the exit gate. "You pulled off another terrific round."

"Thanks." Jina smiled, and her shoulders suddenly felt lighter. "But it was all Superstar," she added, giving him a pat. "He stayed cool, calm—"

"We found it, we found it!" someone called excitedly.

Jina turned in her saddle. Andie, Mary Beth, and Lauren were weaving through the crowd of horses. Andie waved a girth. *Her* girth.

"We looked all over," Mary Beth said breathlessly as they came up. "Lauren finally found it in the cab of Dorothy's pickup, underneath a cooling sheet."

"What was it doing there?" Jina asked. Swinging her right leg over Superstar's rump, she dropped lightly to the ground.

Andie shook her head. "Well, *I* didn't put it there."

"You lost your girth?" Todd asked, puzzled.

Jina nodded. "That's why I was late."

"She didn't *lose* it," Lauren said. Looking around to make sure no one was listening, she whispered, "Somebody took it."

"Huh?" Jina and Todd said together.

"Well, what else could have happened?" Andie asked. "I know I buckled your girth on your saddle."

"Do you think someone was playing a joke?" Jina asked, frowning.

Andie snorted, "No way. Someone wanted you to get all stirred up."

"Yeah, and it worked," Mary Beth chimed in. "Andie said you were—"

"Shut up, Finney," Andie said.

"You mean you girls think that one of the other riders hid Jina's girth?" Todd repeated, frowning. "That's a ridiculous idea."

Andie, Mary Beth, and Lauren looked unconvinced.

Mary Beth leaned closer. "I bet it was Ashley Stewart."

Jina sucked in her breath. Ashley was competitive, all right, but would she stoop to such a mean trick?

Looking around, Jina spotted Ashley and April Fool. They were waiting to jump in the warm-up class. As always, the pretty, older girl was surrounded by her gang of friends.

"She even looks guilty," Mary Beth whispered in her ear. "And Lauren *swears* she saw her earlier by Dorothy's truck."

"Maybe Ashley did hide it. But I really don't care. I shouldn't have lost my cool," Jina said. Dropping her gaze, she stared at the reins in her hands. "Andie, I'm really sorry—"

"Forget it," Andie interrupted. "Just concentrate on winning this championship. Then you can quit worrying about that stupid Horse of the Year Award."

Todd shook his head. "This is too much for me. I've got to help some of my other riders. I'll meet you at the warm-up ring before your next class, Jina."

Andie took the reins from Jina. "Come on, Superstar. Let's cool you off and clean the mud off your legs before you have to get your blue ribbon."

Clucking to the horse, she led him down the gravel drive toward the Foxhall van. Mary Beth, Jina, and Lauren followed.

Jina took off her helmet and wiped the sweat from her forehead. She already felt exhausted and it was only her first class. Suddenly, she stopped in her tracks. A white limo was cruising down the drive toward the show grounds.

Her mother was here!

"Look at that," Mary Beth said. "Do you think some big shot's coming to watch the show?"

"Nah," Andie scoffed. "Probably some rich kid's parents."

The limo slowed as it approached the line of trailers. Jina's heartbeat quickened as the long white car pulled into an empty parking space across from the Foxhall vans.

Lauren turned and looked at Jina. "Hey, didn't a white limo like that one bring you to school the first day?"

"Uh, yeah," Jina stammered.

"Oh my gosh!" Mary Beth gasped.

"What?" Andie and Lauren exclaimed.

Mary Beth pointed at the limo. A woman was getting out of the backseat. She was tall and gorgeous with smooth black skin, and she wore a full-length suede coat.

"That's Myra Golden!" Mary Beth sputtered.

"Myra Golden?" Lauren repeated in disbelief. "The talk show host? The one who interviews people with weird problems?"

Mary Beth nodded emphatically.

"Wow, you're right! That *is* Myra Golden." Lauren gasped. "I wonder why she's here?"

Andie stopped and looked back at the others. "Maybe she's doing a show about horses. You know, 'Why I Let My Horse Live in My Kitchen.' Come on, let's go find out."

"Wait!" Jina blurted out. "I already know why she's here."

All of her roommates turned around. Three pairs of eyes stared at her in surprise.

Jina sighed. Everyone would find out soon enough. "She's here to see *me*. Myra Golden is my mother."

Jina braced herself for her roommates' reactions.

"Myra Golden is your *mother*?" Andie exclaimed.

"I can't believe it!" Mary Beth said excitedly. "*Myra Golden Live* is my mom's favorite show!"

"Why didn't you tell us?" Lauren asked, a hurt pout on her lips. "You kept it such a deep, dark secret. I mean, I think it's cool. A mother who's a big TV star."

"Do you think she'll give us her autograph?" Mary Beth chimed in.

Jina shrugged. "You'll have to ask her."

"Jinaki! Sweetheart!" Myra Golden was making her way toward the girls, her high heels sinking into the mud and her suede coat flapping behind her.

Scrambling beside her was a young man dressed in khaki slacks and a knit shirt. A baseball cap was pulled low on his forehead.

"Hi, Mom." Jina rushed to give her a hug. Her mother enveloped her in soft, leather-clad arms. She smelled like expensive perfume.

"Baby, you look great!" Ms. Golden said, inspecting her daughter from head to toe. "Did I miss your first class?"

"Well, yes. But that's okay."

Myra looked over Jina's head. "Oh, there's Superstar!" she exclaimed. Digging in her coat pocket, she pulled out an apple. "I saved this from breakfast."

"Mom, you shouldn't feed him when he has his bridle on," Jina said quickly, but Myra had already given him the apple.

"And who are these lovely girls?" Ms. Golden asked, her gaze sweeping from Andie to Lauren to Mary Beth. The three girls hadn't said a word. They were staring dumbly at Jina's mom, their mouths hanging open.

"These are my roommates from school," Jina said. It was happening already. Her friends were so awed by Myra Golden that they'd forgotten everything else.

Ms. Golden clapped her palms together. "I'm delighted to meet you girls. Jinaki has told me so much about you. Let's see." She frowned and stepped back to study them.

"You must be Andie, the wild one." Ms. Golden pointed a long, scarlet-red fingernail at Andie. Jina couldn't believe it when Andie actually blushed. "Jinaki told me all about Magic, and how you rode without permission and got in trouble."

"Mom!" Now it was Jina's turn to blush.

Next Jina's mother cupped her fingers around her chin and scrutinized Lauren. "Lauren, right? The little one who has a crush on Todd?"

Lauren's cheeks turned bright red, and she stared down at her toes.

Myra leaned closer. "Don't worry, honey, I understand all about crushes." Then she turned to Mary Beth.

"And that leaves Mary Beth. I bet you're the one who's so afraid of horses."

Mary Beth clapped her hands to her mouth.

"Well, not *totally*," she said, giggling.

Ms. Golden winked. "You don't have to

pretend with me, honey. I'm a little scared of them myself."

"And I'm Jamison," the young man introduced himself. "Myra's administrative assistant." Stepping forward, he shook hands with Lauren, Andie, and Mary Beth.

"Oh, this is so lovely," Myra said. Whirling in a circle, she gazed over the show grounds. Her hair was cropped short and long silver earrings dangled to her shoulders.

Beautiful and gracious as always, Jina thought, her shoulders sagging. No wonder everybody paid so much attention to her mother.

Ms. Golden turned to Jina. "When's your next class, baby? I have to leave in two hours and I don't want to miss it."

"Probably in an hour," Jina said.

"You'll get to see Jina get the blue ribbon for her first jumping class," Mary Beth said.

"We don't know that, Mary Beth," Jina protested. "And the class isn't even over yet."

"Ms. Golden, may I have your autograph?" Lauren asked.

"Why certainly, sweetheart. And please call me Myra. Most people do."

Lauren pulled her show program from her

back pocket. She uncrumpled it and handed it to Myra, who quickly scribbled a signature.

"All I have is my arm," Mary Beth said, holding it out.

Jina's mother laughed. "It won't be the first arm I've autographed."

"Ms. Golden!" the chauffeur called as he hobbled up. "A call for you."

Myra waved him away. "Jamison, you take it."

"But they want you," the chauffeur said.

Myra sighed. "I'm going to have to yank out that car phone. It's *so* annoying." She patted Jina on the shoulder. "I'll be right back, baby."

"Sure," Jina said. She was used to her mother being called away for work.

Jamison followed Ms. Golden to the car. Mary Beth, Lauren, and Andie watched them go, their eyes wide with awe.

Jina turned to the chauffeur. "Hi, Charles."

"Hi, Miss Jina," Charles said. He wagged one finger at her. "You're going to do a good job today, right? You know how much your mama likes to see you win."

Jina nodded, and Charles joined Jamison and her mother back at the limo. Myra's long legs stuck out the open back door. Hovering over her, Jamison listened intently to the phone conversation.

"Wow." Mary Beth broke the silence. "She autographed my arm."

Andie snorted. "It's just going to wash off."

"I wish my mom were that gorgeous," Lauren said.

"And that famous," Mary Beth added. "It must be neat having a star for a mom."

"Yeah, really neat," Jina muttered, swatting Superstar on the neck. Just then the announcer announced the winners of the warm-up class. In all the excitement, Jina had almost forgotten about it.

"You won!" Lauren squealed when Jina's number was called first.

Andie handed the reins to Jina. "Boy, your mom will be proud."

"Let's hope she even notices," Jina said. Her mother was still talking on the phone.

Turning Superstar around, Jina jogged him toward the ring. She could see clusters of girls staring curiously at the limo. When Jina went past them, their eyes seemed to follow her.

"Is she really Myra Golden's daughter?" she heard someone say.

Jina's shoulders slumped. It was going to

start all over again. There was no turning back.

From now on, she'd never know whether the other girls liked her for herself, or because her mother was Myra Golden. Never again would she just be Jina Williams. She'd always be that famous TV star's daughter.

"Okay, Jina. That blue ribbon you won in the warm-up class proved you can do it," Todd said. He stood by Jina's right boot leg. She was mounted on Superstar, waiting to jump in Junior Hunter Over Fences.

"Jina? Are you listening?"

"Hmm?" Jina hadn't heard a word. She was too busy watching her mother.

Myra Golden was leaning against the white board railing around the show ring. Smiling and chattering happily, she signed autographs for the eager crowd of people surrounding her.

Jina sighed. Everyone loved her mother.

Todd tapped her boot. "I said, Jina, you'd better pay attention to your riding or you're going to blow this show."

Jina pulled her gaze away from her mother. "Sorry. I just can't concentrate."

"I don't blame you," Todd said. "Your mom has always been a showstopper. But she's here to see you ride, so show her what *you* can do."

"What difference does it make?" Jina said angrily. "No matter what I do, I'll never be as wonderful as Myra Golden."

For a moment, Todd didn't say anything. Then he gave Jina's boot a squeeze. "Then you'll just have to be as wonderful as Jina Williams can be."

"I guess." Jina looked back at her mother and her fans. Even Mary Beth, Lauren, and Andie were in the crowd.

Oh, quit feeling sorry for yourself, Jina told herself. *So what if your roommates went bonkers over your mother. You expected it, right?*

"Jina," Todd said in his no-nonsense trainer's voice. "You're jumping next. Deep breaths. Big smile. Limber your shoulders. You're stiff as a board."

Jina forced herself to smile. She gathered up the reins and nudged Superstar with her heels, signaling him it was time to wake up.

He shifted beneath her, his muscles tensing in anticipation. Ears pricked alertly, he waited for her next command.

"Jumping next is number thirty-nine, Superstar, owned and ridden by Jinaki Williams."

Loud shouts and cheering sounded from

the area where her mother was standing.

"Good luck!" Todd called as Jina and Superstar went through the entry gate.

You can do it, Jina told herself. *One perfect jump.* She circled Superstar at a trot, then squeezed him into a canter, her eyes and mind focused on the painted stone fence.

"Go baby!" Myra's voice cut through her concentration. "Win this one for me!"

Jina's fingers tightened on the reins.

Win a big one for me!

She had to do it. To show everyone that she wasn't just Myra Golden's daughter. To show her mother that *she* was a winner, too.

Superstar cantered toward the first jump. Jina willed her mind and body to relax, to move with Superstar as if they were one.

He took off, sailing over the fence. Jina leaned forward, balanced over his neck, her hands set lightly below his crest. His front hooves hit the ground and he cantered smoothly to the next fence.

Win this one for me!

Jina couldn't clear her mind. What if she didn't win? What would everyone say?

Suddenly, the third jump was right in front of them. Superstar cleared it easily, but he landed too close. She squeezed him forward, trying to get him into the right stride before the fourth fence.

His canter lengthened, but he lost impulsion—the energy needed to propel himself over the obstacle. Jina panicked. Her mind went blank.

Quick, she told herself, *think*!

The fence loomed in front of them. Jina tried to collect her horse, but it was too late. She signaled Superstar to take off even though they were too far back.

Win.

He flew over the fence. Jina's heart quickened. Maybe they'd be okay.

But Superstar's hind leg caught the top rail and he landed awkwardly. Head down, he stumbled forward, then slid in the muddy footing. Jina grabbed one of her horse's braids and held tight. Like the champion he was, Superstar caught himself before he fell.

Leaping up, the gray began to canter gamely to the fifth fence. But Jina immediately knew something was wrong. His rhythm was way off.

Superstar was hurt!

"Whoa!" Jinaki pulled Superstar to a halt. Tears pricked her eyes as she jumped down.

Not only had she blown the class, but Superstar was lame!

She ran her hand down the back of his right front leg. Already she could feel heat in his tendon. That could mean a sprain or, even worse, a bow where the tendon was actually torn.

"Number thirty-nine, please clear the course."

Head down, Jina led Superstar toward the exit gate. She didn't want to see the disappointment in her mother's eyes.

When she got outside the ring, Todd rushed up to her. "Is he all right?"

Silently, she shook her head. She was afraid

to say anything in case she burst into tears.

Crouching down, Todd clasped his hand around Superstar's leg. "Let's run some cold water on it. I'll fix an ice wrap."

Mrs. Caufield hurried toward them. "Is Superstar okay?"

"No. He's injured his tendon," Todd said. "Jina was smart to pull him up."

Mrs. Caufield put her hand on Jina's shoulder. Myra, Mary Beth, Lauren, Andie, Jamison, and a sea of people Jina didn't recognize dashed up.

"Oh baby!" Myra pulled Jina to her. "You were doing so great!"

Jina yanked away from her. "I was *not* doing great!" she snapped. "I wasn't concentrating and I pushed him too hard. It's my fault he's hurt. And I've blown everything I worked for this year!"

She glared at her mother and everybody else as if daring them to say anything. They all stared blankly back at her. Jina flushed, embarrassed by her outburst.

It wasn't their fault. She was just so angry at herself she couldn't help it.

Todd was leading Superstar back to the Foxhall van. Jina ran to catch up with him.

"Wait!" Andie called. "I'll help."

"Me too," Lauren chimed in. "You must feel awful, Jina."

Jina didn't answer. She was too miserable to talk to her friends right now. When she reached the van, Todd was unbuckling Superstar's girth.

"I'll do that," she said.

He nodded. "I'll hunt up a bucket and get some cold water. Mrs. Caufield's fixing an ice wrap and calling the vet. We'll leave the wrap on Superstar the whole van ride back to Foxhall. Maybe if we can keep the swelling down..." Todd's voice trailed off as he left to get water.

But Jina knew what he was going to say. *Maybe if they kept the swelling down, Superstar wouldn't be lame.*

Pressing her forehead against Superstar's neck, Jina finally let the tears go. Sobs racked her body. There was no way she'd win today's championship.

She'd blown it.

"Tough break, Williams," a voice said behind her.

Jina's head shot up. Ashley Stewart stood

by the van, her gloved hand holding April Fool's reins.

Jina wiped her eyes.

"I mean, it really was too bad," Ashley repeated. For once, she sounded sincere. But Jina didn't trust the girl.

Ashley clucked to April and led the mare off.

Jina stuck out her tongue at Ashley's back. "You're not sorry," she muttered, wiping her nose on her coat sleeve. "Because now you can win the championship."

"Jina!" Her mother rushed up. "Honey, I'm so sorry. I just finished talking to Todd. He told me you won't finish today's show—and you may not be able to ride Superstar for weeks!"

"That's right," Jina said flatly. Trying to avoid her mother's gaze, she lifted the saddle flap and unbuckled the girth.

Superstar snatched a bite of hay from a bale sitting against the van ramp. He had cocked his knee to keep the weight off his right foot, but Jina was glad to see he wasn't too hurt to eat.

Myra sighed. "I know how hard you were

working toward that hunter award. And I don't want you to give up. I'll buy you another horse, sweetie. You can finish out the season and win anyway."

Jina stared at her mother in astonishment.

Myra waved her hands like two fans. "I know, I know. You *love* Superstar. But we don't have to get rid of him!" Her eyes glowed excitedly.

"We'll get a vet to take care of Superstar, and you and your new horse can go on to win that award thing."

Myra stopped pacing and faced Jina with a pleased expression. When Jina didn't say anything, her mother asked, "So what do you think?"

Jina shook her head wearily. "You don't get it, Mom."

"Get it?" Myra looked confused. "Honey, I know how much winning that award means to you."

Jina pulled the saddle and pad off Superstar's back and plopped them on top of the hay bale. "No, I mean you don't understand how showing Junior Hunters works. I can't just jump on another horse and win that award. Every time I go in the ring, they're judging

Superstar. Not me. *He's* the one that's earned the points toward the year-end award."

For a moment, Myra's face fell. Then she brightened again. "We'll just have to find a vet to fix his leg!"

"Cold H_2O coming up," Todd said as he headed toward them, carrying a brimming bucket.

"Ms. Golden!" Charles called, coming up behind Todd. "Mr. Jamison says that if you don't leave now, you'll be late for that taping."

"Tell Jamison to hold his horses," Ms. Golden told the chauffeur brusquely. "I'll be right there."

"Yes ma'am," he replied politely. Then he turned to Jina. "I'm sorry about what happened, Miss Jina. You and your horse looked so pretty jumping all those fences."

Jina smiled gratefully. "Thanks, Charles," she said, but he was already heading back to the car.

Jina turned her attention back to Superstar.

"Give me your hoof, you big clod," Todd was growling from the other side of the gray. He was trying to get the horse to place his foot into the bucket.

"Let me help," Jina said. She glanced over

79

her shoulder, at her mom. "You'd better go before Jamison loses his cool. I've got to help Todd anyway."

"Are you sure?" Ms. Golden asked anxiously.

Jina nodded. "I'm sure."

Her mother reached out and touched Jina's cheek. "I'll call you tomorrow and find out how Superstar is. It'll be okay, baby. You'll see."

Jina forced a smile. "Sure, Mom." Maybe it would be okay.

Jina's mother blew Jina a kiss. Then she started walking briskly to the limo, her high heels crunching in the gravel.

I love you, Mom, Jina told her silently, watching her go.

Then Dorothy strode up with an ice wrap, and Mrs. Caufield hurried over with a support bandage for Superstar's left leg.

Jina didn't have a chance to wave good-bye to her mother. She was already gone.

"It looks like a mid bow," Dr. Holden announced to Dorothy and Jina late that afternoon. The vet was crouched on the concrete floor of the new barn, inspecting the swelling in the back of Superstar's right foreleg.

Dorothy had driven Jina and Superstar back to Foxhall in the trailer. When they arrived at the school, the vet had been waiting.

Jina held Superstar's lead line. She was still dressed in her breeches and black boots. Her hunt coat and helmet were thrown on top of her tack trunk.

"I'm going to use ultrasound to get a sonogram of the tendon," Dr. Holden continued. "That'll tell us just how bad it is." Looking up, he grinned reassuringly at Jina. "It might be just a sprain."

"If it *is* a sprain, how long will Superstar be laid up?" Jina asked, feeling hopeful.

Dr. Holden shrugged. "As long as it takes for it to heal."

He stood up and wiped his hands on his coveralls. "Let me get my portable scanner. Dorothy, you'll have to shave his leg."

Dorothy nodded. "I'll get the clippers."

When the vet went out to his truck, the barn manager turned to Jina. "You look exhausted. I'll help Dr. Holden. Why don't you get some dinner?"

Jina shook her head. "No. I want to watch."

Dorothy nodded, then left to get the clippers. The stable was suddenly quiet. All the other girls were still at the show.

Jina laid her cheek against Superstar's neck and stroked his velvety muzzle. "It's going to be okay," she told him.

The grind of a motor made her glance toward the open aisle door. One of the Foxhall vans was roaring up the drive, kicking gravel dust everywhere.

Someone rolled down the passenger window and waved. It was Andie. Jina could just make out Mary Beth and Lauren in the back, squished together like sardines.

Minutes later, her roommates charged down the aisle.

"How's Superstar?" Lauren asked breathlessly.

"Dr. Holden's not sure. He's using ultrasound to see how much damage there is."

Just then the vet came down the aisle carrying several small black cases. Dorothy followed with a pair of clippers.

Head high, Superstar watched alertly. Lauren, Andie, and Mary Beth moved against the wall to make room.

"Does the ultrasound thing hurt?" Mary Beth whispered to Jina.

Jina shook her head. "No, I saw it done on a horse at Middlefield once. It's just a way of looking at the tendons and muscles of the leg. Kind of like an X ray, but they use sound waves instead."

Dr. Holden began unpacking the cases while Dorothy clipped the back of Superstar's lower leg. Jina watched in silence, wondering what the sonogram would show.

Half an hour later, the veterinarian was moving a transducer—which looked like a flashlight on a cord—up and down Superstar's leg. At the same time, he studied what looked like a small TV screen. A whitish-gray cone showed up on the monitor.

"That's Superstar's leg?" Lauren asked, looking at the wedge-shaped picture.

Dr. Holden nodded, then pointed to the screen. "This shows there's a slight tear in the tissue."

"Is that good or bad?" Jina asked hesitantly.

"Good, because the tear's not severe. We caught it in time, so Superstar should recover fully," Dr. Holden told the group. Then he directed his gaze to Jina. "And bad, because it means he's going to be laid up for four to six months."

Six months? Jina was so stunned she didn't know what to say. Not only was her horse finished for this show season, but a six-month layup meant she couldn't ride him again until late spring. He wouldn't be ready for next year's season either!

Tears filled Jina's eyes. She was happy Superstar would be all right. But her whole last year had centered around showing—and *winning*. One bad jump had changed all that. She might as well face it.

She was a failure.

• • •

Late that night, Jina lay in bed, listening to Andie's muffled snoring and Mary Beth's occasional wheezing.

Tears rolled down her cheeks, leaving a cool trail on her skin. Quickly, she wiped them away with the edge of her comforter.

She couldn't stop thinking about Superstar. Over and over her mind replayed that jump. If only she'd been paying more attention. If only she hadn't been so worried about what her mother would think. If only she hadn't been so set on winning the championship.

If only—if only—

Trying to shut out the haunting words, Jina threw the comforter over her head.

Just then, Lauren turned over in her bed. Jina held her breath. She didn't want anyone to know she was still awake.

"Jina? Are you all right?" Lauren whispered from her corner of the room.

Jina lowered the comforter. "Yeah. I guess."

"I mean, it's okay if you want to cry. Considering what happened and all." Lauren hesitated. "And Jina, it wasn't your fault," she added. "You know that, don't you?"

Jina sniffed. "Y-yes." She plucked a tissue from the box by her bed and blew her nose.

"I don't know what I'd do if that happened to me," Lauren continued. "Cry for a week, maybe."

"A week?" Jina stifled a laugh.

"What so funny about that?"

"There'd be so many tears, you'd flood the dorm. We'd probably all float away."

Lauren laughed, too, and Jina began to feel a little better. She yawned and her eyelids suddenly felt heavy.

"Todd was really cool today, wasn't he?" Lauren asked.

"Mmm," Jina said. "He knew exactly what to do when Superstar hurt himself."

Lauren sighed. "I guess he *is* too old for me. But it's all right for me to like him, don't you think?"

"Sure," Jina mumbled. She wasn't really sure what Lauren had asked her. After a few more minutes of listening to Lauren's happy chatter, she fell into a deep sleep.

"I was very impressed with your first reports," Ms. Thaney told the class as she passed the history papers back on Monday morning.

"However," the teacher went on, "some extra work is in order on bibliographies. I made some corrections, but this time they weren't included in your grade."

Jina swallowed hard as Ms. Thaney walked down the rows. When Mary Beth opened the front cover of her report, Jina could just make out the red A written on the bottom.

"Read over the comments, then see me if you have any questions," Ms. Thaney continued. She stopped at Jina's desk and laid her report on top of Jina's textbook.

Jina held her breath, afraid to open it. She knew she hadn't tried her best. Gingerly, she grasped the corner of the top sheet and slowly peeled it back. A red C blasted back at her.

Quickly, Jina flipped the top page closed.

A C!

She couldn't remember the last time she'd gotten a C. Maybe never.

"Any questions?" Ms. Thaney scanned the room. Jina dropped her gaze.

"So what did you guys get?" Mary Beth asked Lauren, Andie, and Jina when class was dismissed. "I got an A."

"Me too." Lauren beamed proudly. "If I could just do half as well in math," she added with a sigh.

"Well?" Mary Beth prompted Andie and Jina.

Andie scowled.

She didn't get such a hot grade, either, Jina thought.

But then Andie let out a loud whoop. "I got an A too!"

"Give me five!" Mary Beth hooted, and the two girls slapped palms.

"So Jina, what did you get?" Lauren pressed.

"I got a C," Jina mumbled.

"You're kidding!" Andie exclaimed. "You never get C's. Let me see that." She grabbed the paper from Jina.

"Hey, give me that." Jina reached for the report, but her roommate had already opened it and was skimming the first page.

Andie looked up at her. "You did get a C. And Thaney wants to see you."

"She does?" Jina snatched the report back. In big red letters, Ms. Thaney had written, "Please see me after class."

Jina's cheeks grew hot. She didn't need this. Not after her miserable weekend.

"Uh-oh," Andie said under her breath. Jina shot her an angry look. She knew what Andie was thinking. Thaney had found out about the fake sources.

"Good luck," Lauren said. "We'll see you at riding."

"Yeah." Jina tucked the report in her books and turned back toward the classroom. Ms. Thaney was correcting papers at her desk.

"Hello, Jina," the teacher greeted her.

"What did you want to see me about?" Jina asked.

"Oh, yes. About your bibliography."

Jina's stomach somersaulted.

"If you had trouble finding three sources for your report, Jina, you should have come to me," the teacher said. She took off her glasses and laid them on the desk top.

Jina's heart began to race.

"Instead of making the books up," Ms. Thaney continued. Her gaze drilled into Jina's. "Because that's called cheating."

12

"Um, I—" Jina stammered. She didn't know what to say to Ms. Thaney. Making up those last two books had been such a stupid thing to do. Why had she ever listened to Andie?

"I know it was dumb," she said finally. "But the report was late and I didn't have time to talk to you." She looked down at the floor. "I'm really sorry. I've never done anything like that before."

Ms. Thaney nodded. "Luckily, I didn't grade the bibliographies this time. Otherwise you would have gotten an F. But I did have to mark you down for only using one source of information. It made your report biased." She folded her fingers into a steeple. "So, the next time you have problems, you'll let me know?"

"Yes." Jina clutched her books to her chest.

"And Jina, I was sorry to hear about your horse."

"How did you know about Superstar?" Jina asked in surprise.

Ms. Thaney smiled. "Foxhall is a small school, remember? And I am your adviser."

"Oh. Well, thanks."

"You're welcome. And come see me if you need to talk. I don't know much about horses, but I'm a very good listener."

Jina thanked her teacher again and hurried out of the classroom. As soon as she reached the hall, she let out her breath. That had gone better than she'd expected. Ms. Thaney had been pretty nice about the whole thing.

Then Jina frowned. Had her teacher given her special treatment? Was she being extra-understanding because of Superstar's injury? Or because she was Myra Golden's daughter?

"So what did Thaney want to talk to you about?" Andie asked that afternoon.

"You should know," Jina snapped as she flicked the brush roughly over Superstar's back.

The four roommates were standing in the aisle of the new barn. Andie, Lauren, and

Mary Beth had stopped in to see how Superstar was doing before they cleaned their own horses. The gray was hooked to crossties while Jina brushed him. An ice wrap was on his right leg.

It was early afternoon.

"Look, why don't you just tell me what happened?" Andie said.

Jina whirled to face her. "Your stupid idea to make up those sources for the bibliography got me in trouble, that's what."

Andie shrugged. "So why blame me? It's not like I forced you to cheat."

"You cheated?" Lauren said, looking shocked.

"With Andie's so-called help." Jina flushed angrily as she picked up a mane comb from her grooming box. She could see Mary Beth on Superstar's other side, staring down at his front leg.

Lauren crossed her arms. "What Andie did was rotten, Jina, but you have to admit she's right. You didn't have to do it."

Jina stopped combing Superstar's mane. "So it's all my fault?"

"Well, yes," Lauren said.

"And I bet you think Superstar's accident

was all my fault, too, right?" Jina demanded.

"Of course not," Lauren protested.

"Where'd you get that idea?" Andie asked.

Jina ignored them and stomped around to Superstar's other side.

Her insides were churning. Lauren was right. She shouldn't have cheated. It was her own fault. And so was Superstar's injury.

Mary Beth pointed to the gray's right foreleg. "Is the ice wrap helping?"

"Nothing's going to help," Jina muttered.

Mary Beth tilted her chin up. "You sure are in a rotten mood."

"Come on, Finney," Andie called from the other side. "I'm going to watch Dorothy give Magic his eye medication, and you and Lauren need to tack up your horses."

The three girls started to go. Mary Beth stopped and turned to Jina. "Hey, what happened to your horse really stinks. But don't take it out on us."

With that, she disappeared around Superstar. Jina could hear her roommates whispering together as they left the barn.

Sticking the comb in Superstar's tail, Jina yanked hard. A big wad of hair came out. Superstar swung his hindquarters away from her, then switched his tail. The long hairs whipped across Jina's cheek.

"Ouch, you stupid animal." Jina swatted him on the flank. Startled, Superstar lurched forward.

Great, Williams, Jina muttered to herself. *Now you're even taking things out on your horse.*

Just then Ashley Stewart walked up. "Hi, Jina," she said in a fakey nice voice.

Double great. Saturday, Ashley had won the Junior Hunter Championship at Auburn. She was probably there to gloat.

Jina stopped combing and looked up at the older girl. Ashley stood beside Superstar, one hand absently stroking his neck. She wore her riding helmet and leather chaps over her jeans.

"What do *you* want?" Jina grabbed Superstar's tail and started combing furiously.

Ashley raised her eyebrows. "Take it easy," she said. "I just want to know how your horse is doing."

Sure you do, Jina thought. "Better than yours," she said aloud. "Even when he's lame."

To Jina's surprise Ashley laughed. Then the older girl added, "You know, I was thinking. Now that Myra Golden—your mom is Myra, right?"

Jina combed harder. Ashley knew exactly who her mother was.

"Well, anyway, since rich and famous Myra can't buy you another win, you're just like everyone else," Ashley continued. "And it's making you mad, isn't it? That's why you're so nasty to your horse."

Jina's cheeks burned. "I swatted my horse because he switched me in the face," she retorted.

"Whatever you say." Smiling knowingly, Ashley tucked a lock of blond hair under the brim of her helmet. "You spent all year busting your breeches to win. And now you're through."

"Winning isn't everything," Jina said, clenching her teeth.

Ashley arched one brow. "Oh really? I bet you like to win more than anything in the world," she said. "Too bad it won't be this year." Giving Superstar one last pat, she strode off down the aisle.

During dinner that night, Jina ate silently. At the table to her right, Lauren, Mary Beth, and Andie huddled over their trays, still whispering together.

Jina tried to ignore them as she shoveled

macaroni and cheese into her mouth. She told herself it was just bad luck that she'd been assigned to a different table this week. Or maybe it was good luck.

She could tell they were talking about her. Their eyes kept darting in her direction.

The minute Headmaster Frawley dismissed the students, Jina jumped up. Without a backward glance, she marched from the cafeteria.

When she reached the suite, she grabbed her English lit book. Then she kicked off her moccasins and threw herself on the bed. She had so much to do before the next horse show on Saturday.

Jina caught herself.

There was no show for her on Saturday. That meant no tack to clean, no extra lessons with Todd, no boots to polish. She had all the time in the world to get her homework done.

With a sigh, Jina let the book fall across her face.

The suite door opened. Jina peeked out from behind her book just as Lauren stepped inside the room and shut the door behind her.

She had a funny look on her face.

"What's the matter with you?" Jina asked.

"Me?"

"Who else would I be talking to?" Jina knew she sounded rude, but she didn't care.

"Right. Ha-ha." Lauren grinned. "Nothing's the matter."

"Where are Mary Beth and Andie? They'll be late for study time."

Lauren's gaze shot to the closed door. "They're, uh—" She bit her lip, then blurted— "They're talking to Ms. Shiroo!"

Jina sat up. "Why?"

"I don't know," Lauren said with a shrug.

Jina frowned. Something was definitely up. Lauren was such a bad liar. But why would Andie and Mary Beth be talking to the dorm mother?

Then it hit her.

Mary Beth, Lauren, and Andie didn't want her as a roommate anymore!

13

Jina stared at Lauren, horrified. Her roommates wanted to get rid of her!

"Jina? Are you all right?" Lauren's grin faded.

"What do you care?" Jina cried. She jumped off the bed. "Now I know what you guys have been whispering about for the last two days. You don't want me to be your roommate anymore!"

Jina grabbed her bathrobe and shower bucket, and stormed into the bathroom.

Lauren pounded on the door. "Jina? What are you talking about?"

"Oh, go away!" Jina stuck her fingers in her ears, but she could still hear Lauren. Reaching into the shower stall, she turned on the water full blast.

Then she jumped in and let the water blast into her face.

She'd show them. First thing in the morning, she'd go to Ms. Shiroo and tell her she wanted to move out of suite 4B.

Tears mingled with the stinging spray. She really didn't want to move. Sure, Lauren was nosy, Mary Beth was clueless about horses, and Andie was bossy. But they were also lots of fun.

She liked her roommates a lot. But she couldn't blame them if they didn't like her.

Jina turned off the shower and listened for noises outside the bathroom door. It was quiet. Lauren must have left.

Slowly, Jina dried herself, then brushed her teeth and packed up her shower bucket. She slipped her flannel nightie over her head and opened the bathroom door. The room was empty.

Maybe she'd go ahead and start packing. Then her roommates would think she'd planned to move all along.

With a heavy heart, Jina pulled her suitcase from under her bed. It still held sweaters and pants that she hadn't been able to stuff in the drawers. Her mother always insisted on buying her way too many clothes.

She was rearranging the clothes, when she heard the door to the suite open. She pretended not to notice.

"I told you," Lauren said, in a loud whisper.

"Okay, okay, you were right," Andie replied.

Three pairs of feet walked into the suite. The door shut. Jina kept her eyes on her suitcase, but her heart was thumping. How were her roommates going to break the news to her?

"Jina, we didn't want to tell you this because—" Lauren began, then hesitated.

"Because it will totally *ruin* everything," Mary Beth chimed in.

Lauren cleared her throat. "But when you went kind of nuts a few minutes ago, we decided we had to tell you."

"Tell me what?" Jina asked, her heart pounding.

Andie sighed. "About the surprise party we're having for you."

Another disastrous party in the Common Room? Jina wondered.

"*We're* not really having it," Lauren explained. "Your mother is. Andie and Mary Beth were just talking to your mom on the phone."

Jina sat back on her bare heels. "That's what you guys have been whispering about? A party?"

Her roommates nodded.

"But my riding season is over," Jina said. "What is there to celebrate?"

"Your birthday, dummy," Mary Beth said. "You're going to be twelve on Saturday, remember?"

"And you've been so down since Superstar got hurt that we thought we should do something to cheer you up," Lauren put in.

Andie grinned. "You know how much we love parties."

"We wanted this to be a big deal," Mary Beth added. "So yesterday Andie called your mom to invite her. She said she'd planned on a quiet dinner with you, but when she heard how depressed you were, she thought a party was a great idea. She's hiring a—oof."

Andie had jabbed Mary Beth in the ribs. "Quiet, big mouth," she hissed.

"But I just talked to my mom yesterday," Jina said, frowning. "She didn't say a thing about a party."

Andie rolled her eyes. "That's because it was supposed to be a *surprise*."

"Oh." Jina looked down at the open suitcase. She felt so stupid!

Lauren crouched next to her. "Did you really think we didn't want you to be our roommate anymore?"

Jina flushed, then nodded.

Mary Beth flopped onto Jina's bed. "No way! You *have* been a pain since Saturday, but if we can put up with Andie, we can put up with anyone!"

Andie threw Jina's pillow at Mary Beth's head.

"So who's going to call Jina's mother and tell her the party's not a surprise?" Lauren asked.

Mary Beth and Andie pointed at each other.

"I'll tell her." Jina closed her suitcase and stood up. "It's my fault you guys had to blow it. But I'm glad you did," she added quickly. "I was really sure..." her voice trailed off.

"No way," Lauren said firmly. "The girls in suite 4B have got to stick together."

For the first time since Saturday, Jina gave her roommates a real smile. Things were beginning to look up!

• • •

"Hey, Andie, Magic's doing great!" Jina called from her perch on the fence rail. It was Tuesday afternoon, and Andie was leading the handsome mahogany-colored horse around the back pasture. A chain was looped through the halter rings and over his nose for better control.

"Dr. Holden was here this morning," Andie said as she and Magic walked closer.

Jina peered at Magic's left eye. It looked perfectly normal.

"He says as far as he can tell, the operation was successful," Andie went on. "In one more week I should be able to turn him out in a small pasture."

The wind rustled through the leaves. Magic stopped and snorted loudly, his coat glistening in the afternoon sun.

"Looks like he's really full of himself," Jina said, with a laugh. "I'm glad *I'm* not going to be the first person to ride him."

"Don't worry," Andie said. "Mrs. Caufield and I have mapped out a great retraining program for Mr. Magic here. This afternoon she's teaching me how to longe. That way, when Magic's ready, I can work him first on the longe line. By the time I ride him, he should be dead quiet. I can hardly wait."

Jina sighed. "I wish *I* could ride again."

Andie halted Magic in front of Jina. "How much longer do you think it will be before you can ride Superstar? The swelling is starting to go down, right?"

Jina nodded. "He's not lame anymore, but that's because he's taking anti-inflammatory pills. Dr. Holden's going to do another sonogram on him in two weeks to see if the tendon's healing. It's going to be a long time before he can be ridden."

"That's too bad. What are you going to do?"

"I don't know." Jina said. She wasn't that sure that she would ever ride again. It was all too painful.

Magic pawed the ground, eager to get moving.

"I'd better keep walking him," Andie said. "Don't you have to walk Superstar?"

"Yeah," Jina said, sighing again. Lately it had been hard to even look at her injured horse.

"See you later, then." Andie waved, then turned her attention back to Magic, who was prancing sideways.

Jina jumped to the ground and walked up

the hill to the barns, taking a detour past the riding ring. Mary Beth and Dan were trotting in a small circle around Dorothy. Jina was surprised to see that Mary Beth wasn't on the longe line.

She grinned at the determined expression on her roommate's face as she and Dan jogged down the side of the ring. It had taken Mary Beth three weeks to get up the nerve to trot alone. But at least she'd done it.

Reluctantly, Jina headed toward the new barn. She knew Superstar was waiting for her. Dorothy had walked him in the morning, but it was Jina's job in the afternoon.

She waved to Lauren, who was mounted on Whisper. The two were walking down the drive toward the indoor ring. Katherine Parks walked beside them, gesturing animatedly.

They're probably talking about the dressage competition, Jina thought. *Everybody has a goal they're working toward. What am I going to do?*

Did she really want to quit riding?

"Jina!" Mrs. Caufield called. She was rushing through the office door, smiling broadly. "Todd just called. He has exciting news!"

14

"What did Todd say?" Jina asked eagerly.

The riding director beamed. "One of Todd's clients bought a large pony for their daughter. The pony's green, but he has lots of potential. They want to try him out at a couple of end-of-the-season shows. And they want *you* to ride him!"

"What about their daughter?" Jina asked, frowning. "Doesn't she want to ride him?"

"Todd says she's not ready to show a green pony yet."

Jina shook her head. "I don't know. Why do they want me?"

Mrs. Caufield looked surprised. "Jina, you're an excellent rider. And you're small enough to show a large pony. Besides, even though the jumps are lower, the Pony Hunter divisions are just as competitive as Junior Hunter, so it'd be good experience for you. You can't spend the rest of the semester walking Superstar."

"Oh." Why wasn't she excited about this idea? She'd be showing again, working with Todd—"Thanks, but I don't think so, Mrs. Caufield," Jina said finally. "I'd rather do something else for the riding program."

"May I ask why?" Mrs. Caufield raised her eyebrows.

Jina swallowed hard. "I just don't want that much pressure again. I mean, that's why Superstar got hurt. I was so anxious about winning and points—I blew it." She looked down at her boots. "I'm sorry."

"Don't be sorry." Mrs. Caufield folded her arms. "But this would be different. Todd doesn't expect the pony to win. He just wants to give him experience at the shows." She shaded her eyes and looked down the drive, "Todd's bringing the family to meet you—I bet that's them now."

"Here?" Jina spun around. A silver Mercedes was barreling toward the stable.

Jina watched in growing horror as the car stopped. A girl about seven years old emerged from the back. A few moments later, Todd climbed out of the passenger side, and the little girl ran up and grabbed his hand.

The girl's mother joined them, and the three walked over to Jina and Mrs. Caufield. The little girl bounced with excitement. Her hair was a mess of blond curls, and the knees of her jeans were grass-stained.

By contrast, the mother wore an immaculate blue suit, a paisley-print scarf looped around her neck. Her hair was pulled back in a gold barrette.

Todd grinned at Jina. "Hi there. I thought I'd bring the Chamberses to meet you. Jina Williams, this is Whitney Chambers," he said, looking down at the little girl.

Whitney smiled shyly. Her two front teeth were missing.

"Uh, hi, Whitney," Jina said.

"And this is Whitney's mom."

Jina shook hands with Mrs. Chambers. While Todd introduced Mrs. Caufield, and the three of them started talking about showing, Jina glanced down at Whitney.

"Can I have your autograph?" The little girl blurted out.

"My autograph?" Jina asked, surprised.

Whitney nodded. "Yes. You're such a good rider. And you're going to show Apple!"

"Apple?"

"My pony," Whitney said. "Applejacks." She stuck out her hand, and Jina saw the newspaper clipping of her jumping Superstar clutched in it. "I saved it. For you to sign."

Jina heard Todd choke down a chuckle. She glanced up at him, over at Mrs. Chambers, then down at the little girl.

"Please?" Whitney said.

Todd handed Jina a pen. Holding the photo against her thigh, she wrote her name.

When she gave it back, Whitney carefully folded it and stuck it in her back pocket. Shyly, she stepped closer and slipped her hand into Jina's.

"Will you show me Superstar?" she asked. "Because I think he's the most beautiful horse in the world. Next to Apple, I mean."

Jina shot Todd and Mrs. Caufield a pained look. How could she tell this little girl she didn't want to show her pony?

But Todd and Mrs. Caufield were smiling at her.

Maybe they were right. Since there wouldn't be any pressure on her to win, showing a pony like Applejacks just might be fun.

"Sure you can see Superstar," Jina told Whitney. Holding tight to the little girl's hand, she led her toward the barn. "And then I want you to tell me all about your pony."

"You were able to get a band for my party? On such short notice?" Jina said into the phone.

"Not just *any* band," her mother replied. "The Renegades!"

"The Renegades!" Jina exclaimed, looking over her shoulder at Andie, Lauren, and Mary Beth.

"The Renegades!" She could hear her roommates repeating excitedly as they danced down the hall of the dorm in their stockinged feet. Her mom had hired one of the hottest bands around for her birthday party!

"I thought Andie, Lauren, and Mary Beth could spend the night with us at the hotel suite," Jina told her mom. "All you have to do is call Mrs. Volkert before three on Thursday for permission. She's like the prison guard of overnights, and—"

"Sweetheart," Ms. Golden cut in, "I don't think your roommates can come to the party."

Her mother's words caught Jina by surprise.

"What do you mean they can't come?" she said, lowering her voice so her roommates couldn't hear. "They're the ones who thought of the whole thing!"

"Honey, there's no way I can take responsibility for four girls in a big city like Baltimore. There will be more than a hundred people at the party. It's difficult enough keeping track of you."

Jina's heart sank. Her gaze darted to her roommates. They were huddling in the doorway of suite 4A, telling the other girls from their floor all about the big party.

"Then I don't want to go, either," Jina told her mother. "It won't be any fun if they can't come. Only *your* friends are invited!"

"That's not true, Jinaki," Ms. Golden said sternly. "Grandma Williams and your cousins Tasha and Keem are going to be there. Besides, I've made special arrangements to come and pick you up from Foxhall myself. It will be just you and me the whole ride into Baltimore. We'll have all your favorite snacks and sit and talk for once."

At first, Jina didn't reply. Then she sighed. There was no way she was going to win against her mother. "It's just that—"

"The girls will understand," Ms. Golden said. "The school probably wouldn't allow them to go anyway, without special permission from their parents. And it's a little late for that."

"I guess." Jina's fingers clutched the receiver tightly. Her roommates had really been looking forward to the party. What was she going to tell them?

She said good-bye and slowly hung up. Andie, Lauren, and Mary Beth rushed down the hall toward her, squealing in excitement.

"The Renegades!" Lauren cried.

"Co-o-o-ol!" Andie shouted.

"Um—" Jina began.

"The Renegades aren't coming?" Mary Beth asked quickly.

Jina shook her head numbly. "That's not it."

"There's not going to be a party?" Andie guessed.

Jina cleared her throat. "Worse." She looked down at the floor. "My mother said you guys can't come."

No one said a word. Hesitantly, Jina raised her eyes. Her friends were staring at her with shocked expressions.

Jina swallowed hard. She'd expected

screams of protest, not this awful, hurt silence.

"I'm so sorry." She burst into tears and covered her face with her hands.

Andie put her arm around Jina's shoulders and led her into their suite. "Hey, it's not your fault," she said with false cheeriness. "I mean, moms are like that."

"Yeah." Mary Beth nodded and wiped a tear from her own cheek. "Except my mom always invited my friends."

"Mary Beth!" Lauren poked her in the ribs with her elbow.

Jina sat down on her bed and pulled out a handkerchief. "That's okay," she said, blowing her nose. "Mary Beth's right."

"Well, your mom must have her reasons," Lauren said, sitting down next to Jina.

"She said she wouldn't be able to be responsible for you in a big place like Baltimore, with all those people."

"That sounds like your typical parent explanation," Andie said.

"Well, okay. We can handle that," Lauren said. "Right, Mary Beth? Right, Andie?"

"Right," the two chorused gloomily.

"The important thing is that *you* go and have a good time," Lauren continued, patting

Jina's shoulder. "The party's supposed to cheer you up."

Somehow Jina didn't think it would. Drying her eyes, she looked up at her roommates. "I really am sorry. Did I ever mention that you three are the greatest?"

Andie nodded. "At least a dozen times," she said solemnly. "But we can always hear it again."

Jina checked her watch for the tenth time. It was already after five. Her mom was supposed to have picked her up half an hour ago.

It was Friday afternoon, and she was waiting impatiently in Bracken Hall's front foyer. Her low black heels pinched her feet, the lace on the collar of the new velvet dress was rubbing her neck raw, and the matching green hair band kept slipping.

Lauren and Mary Beth had oohed and aahed over the emerald green party dress her mom had mailed her. It was pretty, and probably cost buckets, but Jina hated it. It looked like something she should've worn for her ninth birthday instead of her twelfth.

"Is she here yet?" Lauren called as she came down the stairs to the foyer.

Jina shook her head.

"Hey, there she is now!" Lauren pointed out the window. The limo was pulling up in front of the dorm.

"Have a great time," Lauren said. "And remember…"

Jina grinned. "I know. Get autographs from every member of the band!"

She waved good-bye and walked out to the waiting limo, her heels clicking on the pavement.

Charles already had the back door open. "Good evening, Miss Jina." He greeted her with a half bow. "You look lovely tonight."

"Thanks, Charles," Jina said shyly.

But when she slid onto the backseat, her mother wasn't there. Jina jumped out just as Charles was about to shut the door.

"Did you forget something?" he asked.

"No!" she said, her eyes snapping angrily. "But it seems that *somebody* has. Where's my mother?"

"Ahhh." Charles's lined face remained unchanged. "She had an unexpected delay. A complication in the party plans that she had to attend to. She tried to call the school, but the lines were busy."

Jina's body tensed. "But she *promised*! She promised we'd have time together during the ride to Baltimore."

"I know," Charles said, nodding. "And she was very upset that she couldn't make it." He gestured toward the limo. "But all your favorite things are in there for you: sour cream chips, a Renegades tape—"

Jina turned away. "I don't want those things," she said between gritted teeth. "I'm not going to the party."

Charles's brows lifted. "But Miss Jina, you *have* to go."

"No I don't." Jina drew herself up taller. "I know this isn't your fault, Charles. Obviously, my mother thought her own stupid party was more important than her daughter. It's probably because I'm not a winner anymore. But I don't care. Please drive back and tell her that I hope she has a great time—without me!"

15

"But Miss Jina!" Charles protested. "I can't tell your mother that!"

"Then make something up!" Jina called over her shoulder. She was already halfway up the sidewalk. Angrily, she wrenched the door open, then slammed it shut behind her.

Three older girls coming down the stairs stared curiously at her. Jina scowled at them, then stomped up the stairs to her room.

"What are *you* doing here?" Lauren asked. She was hunched over on her bed, painting her toenails.

Jina pulled off the green hair band and threw it across the room. "I decided not to go."

"You what?" Mary Beth exclaimed. Dressed in her poodle pajamas, she was playing cards on the floor with Andie.

"All right, Williams!" Andie gave Jina the thumbs-up sign. "You told your mom off!"

Lauren sat bolt upright. "But why aren't you going?"

Jina kicked off her shoes. "Oh, it's a long story."

Andie looked around the suite with a puzzled expression. "Gee. I guess we're too busy to listen. What time were all those cute guys stopping over for pizza and a video?"

Jina threw up her hands. "Okay, okay, I'll tell you. I'm not going because my mother broke her promise."

Lauren swung her legs around to the floor. "What did she promise you? A new horse?"

"A diamond necklace?" Mary Beth guessed.

"Come on guys, get real," Andie scoffed. "She promised Jina a date with one of the Renegades."

Jina half-smiled. "No. Nothing like that. She promised to come with Charles when he picked me up so we'd have the whole ride to talk. Only she didn't."

"Oh, wow." Lauren made a tsking noise. "Super-disappointment."

Andie nodded. "Boy, do I know *that* feeling. My father's done it to me a million times."

"Gee, mine hasn't," Mary Beth said. "But if it was me, I wouldn't miss my birthday party for anything. Especially a big blowout like your mom was planning."

"Yeah, well that's you." Jina pulled off the velvet dress and threw it on the floor.

"Hey, why don't we have our own party?" Lauren suggested.

"Good idea," Andie said. "We don't have the Renegades, but we have some of their tapes."

Lauren jumped off the bed, wads of tissue still stuffed between her newly polished toes. "My mom sent me a care package this morning." She bent down and pulled a box from under the bed. "There's even a mix for a microwave cake. And one of those containers of frosting, too."

"We can get soda and chips out of the snack machine like we usually do," Mary Beth said.

"This will be fun!" Lauren said. "Well, not as much fun for you as your mom's party," she added to Jina quickly.

Jina grinned. "Don't bet on it. But hey, let's make it just the four of us, okay?"

An hour later, the girls were sitting in the

Common Room munching chips and sipping sodas. A delicious smell was wafting from the microwave, and one of Jina's favorite movies was playing on the TV.

When the microwave bell dinged, Lauren jumped up. "We'll have to wait for the cake to cool before we frost it," she told the others.

"No way!" Andie said. "We can just spread globs of icing on top. So what if it melts?"

"I love it that way," Mary Beth said. "Hand me a spoon."

"Spoon?" Andie exclaimed. "Let's use our fingers."

Everyone laughed. Just then, Ashley Stewart sauntered into the Common Room.

Jina glanced at her uneasily. Ashley stopped in front of the soda machine, dropped in her money, and pulled out a diet soda. Then she walked over to the girls.

"Party?" she asked.

"Yeah, and you're not invited," Andie said, without missing a lick of icing.

Ashley snorted. "Like I care. But I do want to talk to Jina."

Jina froze, a spoonful of icing stuck in her mouth.

"I heard you're going to be showing again," Ashley said.

"Large pony," Jina said stiffly.

Ashley nodded. "Well, good luck. I'm glad you're going to be riding again. You should do well."

Jina wasn't sure she'd heard correctly. Was Ashley Stewart complimenting her? "Thanks," she stammered. "Would you like a piece of cake?"

Ashley shook her head. "Too fattening," she said. "But have a good party." She started to leave the room. Then she turned and added over her shoulder, "By the way, I didn't take your girth."

"What was *that* all about?" Mary Beth asked, when the older girl had gone. "Do you believe her?"

Jina shook her head. "I'm not sure."

"Well, if Ashley *didn't* take your girth, who did?" Andie asked, frowning.

"I don't know," Jina said with a sigh. "But it doesn't really matter now."

"Maybe now that you're not competing against her, you and Ashley will get along better," Lauren said.

"Maybe," Jina said. Right now she didn't want to think about Ashley or the girth or showing. "Boy, this cake sure is good," she added. Then a momentary pang made her stop licking. This was the first birthday she'd spent without her mom.

Did her mother miss her, too?

"Hey, should we give Jina her present now?" Mary Beth asked the others.

"Sure," Andie said. She went over to the cupboard and pulled out a wrapped rectangular package. "We went together on it." She handed the present to Jina. Carefully, Jina unwrapped the paper. Inside was a framed photograph of Jina sitting on Superstar.

She was riding him bareback with just a halter. Her gaze was on the camera, and she was smiling happily.

Jina gasped. "Wow, guys. This is the best!"

"Remember when I took that picture?" Mary Beth asked.

Jina nodded. "It was the Monday after that first show we all went to, remember? You guys almost missed it because you had Breakfast Club."

Andie groaned. "How could we forget *that*?"

Jina smiled down at the photo. "Look at

Superstar." Ears pricked, he gazed intently at the camera. "He loves to have people take his picture."

For a moment, she studied the photo, and her heart seemed to swell. In her anger and pain over Superstar's lameness this last week, she'd forgotten how much she loved him—even if he wouldn't win the Horse of the Year Award.

It would be fun riding and showing Applejacks for Whitney Chambers. But she'd never forget that Superstar was her own, special horse.

Tomorrow, I'll have to tell him, she thought, folding the picture against her chest.

A sudden knock on the Common Room door made her jump. Jina spun around.

Her mother was standing in the doorway. Dressed in a silky, shimmering blue dress, she looked like a dream.

Jina blinked her eyes. "Mom? What are you doing here?"

Ms. Golden stepped into the room, an anxious smile on her face. "I heard there was a party going on," she said. "And I was wondering if I could come, too."

"But what about *your* party?" Jina asked.

Her mother shrugged. "Without you, honey, it wouldn't have been any fun. I left Jamison to tell the guests that I had an important appointment."

"Oh." Tears filled Jina's eyes. Her mother *had* missed her!

Still clutching the picture of Superstar, she looked at her friends. "Is it okay if a grown-up comes to our party, guys?"

"Sure!" the girls exclaimed.

Jina looked down at the soggy cake, then back at her mom. "There's even a piece of cake left for you," she said, a sob catching in her throat.

As her mother rushed forward to give her a big hug, Jina thought it might be the best birthday party ever.

**Don't miss the next book
in the Riding Academy series:
#4: LESSONS FOR LAUREN**

"Lauren, what's wrong?" Mary Beth asked anxiously.

Lauren hesitated. She might as well face it. She wasn't going to be able to hide this from her roommates anymore.

"I'm flunking math," she said finally.

There. She'd said it. Now Mary Beth would know what a total dummy she was.

"Flunking?" Mary Beth wrinkled her freckled nose. "You mean, like in a 'D'? Or worse?"

Lauren nodded. "And you know what else it means? If I can't pull my grade up by midterms, I'll have to drop out of the riding program!"

**If you love horses, you'll enjoy
these other books from Bullseye:**

THE BLACK STALLION
THE BLACK STALLION RETURNS
THE BLACK STALLION AND THE GIRL
SON OF THE BLACK STALLION
A SUMMER OF HORSES
WHINNY OF THE WILD HORSES